To Seduce A Lady's Heart

A Landon Sisters Novel

To Seduce A Lady's Heart

A Landon Sisters Novel

INGRID HAHN

Entangled Publishing, LLC
2614 South Timberline Road
Suite 109
Fort Collins, CO 80525
Visit our website at www.entangledpublishing.com.

Scandalous is an imprint of Entangled Publishing, LLC.

Edited by Erin Molta
Cover design by Liz Pelletier
Cover art from Period Images and iStock

Manufactured in the United States of America

First Edition July 2017

For Jonathan, my partner in no crime, because we're too old, too tired, and both much happier being on the right side of the law. And for our little one, Henry, who takes much delight in his crimes, which have only just begun.

Prologue

London, mid-May, near the end of the Season, 1812

The late afternoon was much the same as the others that had preceded it. All thirty, to be precise.

Today would be different. Today he would *not* be turned away.

He had but one final debt to pay. Then he would be free.

Jeremy Landon, Earl of Bennington, pulled his timepiece from a small pocket, opened the lid, nodded in approval, and slipped it away again. He took the steps to Lady Rushworth's white Mayfair terrace house two at a time. The angled sun had turned the facade the color of parchment.

The temperature and weather conditions varied from day to day, as did the color of his waistcoat. Otherwise, the routine was the same.

In the inside pocket of his jacket was the list Jeremy had penned ten years ago, almost to the day. In the last decade, it had been folded, unfolded, and refolded so many times that it was falling apart. It enumerated all the private debts his uncle—his predecessor—had incurred.

Upon his uncle's death, he'd sifted through all the man's papers, painstakingly cataloging every last debt. He had vowed not to overlook a single one. No matter if it was a debt of ten pounds or ten thousand pounds, every penny would be repaid.

The affairs had been in such a state of disorder, the project had taken the better part of a month. And of the many horrors of the situation, the worst was that the previous earl hadn't borrowed solely from faceless creditors. He'd also borrowed from *friends*. Heavily.

Even after all this time, if Jeremy thought about it too long, the whole business made him recoil in disgust.

All the names and debts on his list had been crossed off.

Except one—the strangest of them all. Jeremy had discovered it scrawled in a hastily written note that had been torn into pieces and lost under a pile of neglected papers. When he'd arranged the scraps and deciphered the scrawl, he'd surmised that the late Lord Rushworth had loaned his friend a jewel. Jeremy had spent the last seven years trying to trace it, all the while methodically settling the other debts. He'd hired runners to pry into the affair, but they'd come back with nothing to report. The unnamed stone, whatever it might have been, had vanished.

He'd finally admitted to himself that the jewel would never be recovered. It had taken three years, but Jeremy had finally raised enough to pay what he hoped would approximate the estimated worth of the piece. Plus interest.

Ten years after inheriting a title and an earldom left in disastrous ruin—neither of which he'd wanted—ten years after putting his own life aside and living to restore what his late uncle had lost, he would at last be free. If he could pay what was owed.

Except, thus far Lady Rushworth had obstructed his

attempts.

First, he had sent the money. It'd been returned without any note of explanation. Next, he'd tried working through solicitors. Twice more his money had been returned, letter unopened, banknotes untouched.

He'd delivered it to her house…and found it pinned to his door the next morning, a knife through the center of the packet.

Among other things, Lady Rushworth apparently had a flair for the dramatic.

That was when he'd decided he'd find a way to see her. It was unlikely that she would attempt to run a knife through him. Though the possibility could not be ruled out.

The woman meant to outlast him, but her dogged stubbornness served only to bring out his—the same that had seen him through the trials and tribulations of the last decade.

The woman in question was not unknown in Society. But either she'd stopped venturing out of her home, which he very much doubted, or she made absolutely certain she and he would not be invited to the same gatherings. She didn't go to the park, the theater, or to Bond Street. And Jeremy's blood, earl or not, would never permit him the indulgence of an Almack's voucher.

Enough was enough.

At the door, Jeremy knocked. The now-familiar squinting face of Caruthers allowed him entrance. The ancient butler smelled of caraway seeds and shuffled as he walked.

If the old servant was tired of the routine, he didn't reveal it. On the contrary. He bowed, the picture of stoic propriety. "Your card, my lord?"

"I'm not here to leave a card today, my good man." Jeremy stepped into the entranceway, which was decorated in the latest fashion of airy classicism and bespoke the finest taste.

Caruthers's expression remained placid.

Jeremy, were he a betting man—which he most certainly was not—would have put money on the nonplussed servant having expected such a response. "Today I'm going to see her."

"Her ladyship is not at home."

The devil she wasn't. "I'm terribly sorry. It's not my intention to put you in an awkward position, but I've said it's imperative that I see her, and I'm not in the habit of exaggerating."

Jeremy caught movement from above. On the stairs towering above them was a shadowy figure. She had angular features that might once have been comely but had succumbed to what Jeremy supposed was a lifetime of bitterness.

The woman could have been none other than Lavinia Burke, Countess of Rushworth. Even at a distance, a ruthless gleam shone from her eyes.

It mattered not. This was no social call.

"But you are in the habit of barging in where you're not wanted?"

Lady Rushworth had already made it plain she cared nothing for him or his family. Knowing something of the woman's reputation, he'd expected some resistance. Not complete refusal, however. There was no scenario in Jeremy's mind in which a paid debt—closed and forgotten forever—was not an excellent thing.

In retrospect, that could have been shortsighted. Lady Rushworth's hatred of the Landons was notorious.

The woman could think whatever she wanted. The matter had to be settled once and for all. And so, after nearly a decade away, he'd been forced to return to London and manage the feat himself.

He bowed. "Lady Rushworth, I presume. At long last."

"I would acknowledge you, my lord, but I cannot bring

myself to speak your name." Before he could formulate a response, she continued. "I half expected you to accost me in the street as I went to my carriage."

"I considered the possibility, my lady, but ruled such a maneuver unsporting."

Descending, bejeweled hand on the polished rail, she gave Caruthers a glance. Reading her signal perfectly, the man vanished.

"But pushing your way into my home is acceptable in your code of conduct? I must say, you have much to learn about being a gentleman, my lord. But then, what am I to expect from the likes of a Landon? Disgraceful bunch, the lot of you."

"It's a rule I'm willing to bend to see my task completed."

"Stubbornness, as it were, is not generally a trait of your family. Nor is loyalty—"

"I hate to deprive you the pleasure of your insults, my lady. I give you free rein to despise me, if you will. But I'm here to make reparations. Furthermore, I must ask you not to judge me for who my late uncle was and what he did."

Jeremy had no love for the man, either. However, finding common ground with Lady Rushworth was not the purpose of his visit, nor did he wish to discuss the late earl with anyone. Least of all her.

"If I'm not to judge you for that..." She reached the landing. Close up, she was far more imposing—tall and powerful, with an air of ruthlessness that couldn't have been solely reserved for the likes of him. Pity any weak individual who displeased her. "...then I'm left to judge you for what your actions toward me have been. I'm not certain that's entirely favorable."

"Pray hear me out, my lady."

"Whatever you have to say, I don't want to hear it."

Heedless of her wishes, he pushed on. "I want to make

reparations on my uncle's behalf."

At this, she snorted. "Whatever you think you're about, I assure you, I have no need of *anything* from the likes of *you*."

"I have discharged all my late uncle's debts—all except one. I ask you allow me to pay it. Then you will be rid of me forever."

"To perdition with your repayment, your honor, and your entire family. I curse the day you and your forebears were born."

Although he was unused to such talk, the insults weren't half as maddening as being prevented from doing what was right. Frustration curled hard and tight within him, his muscles clenching.

The two families had once been dear to one another. But Jeremy's uncle's profligate ways had driven them apart. Or so the story went. Jeremy had always wondered if there was something deeper at the heart of the matter.

He'd never been able to discover what it was *precisely* that had driven her ladyship to hold his family in the same esteem as something foul scraped from the gutter. He'd tried asking his aunt once. Though he'd thought he'd been delicate about his phrasing, he'd earned an uncharacteristically sharp rebuke and a reprimand about minding his own affairs.

Now, in the face of Lady Rushworth's provoking words, he had to quell the impulse to inquire. "I understand you don't want anything to do with me, my lady. But I must beg for your compassion—your understanding of my…predicament." That was, his vow to be as different from his uncle as possible. Whatever his uncle did, Jeremy would do the exact opposite. "I *need* this."

A slow smile touched her lips, triumph shining from her expression. She looked, for all the world, as if thwarting him were the culmination of her life's work. "I believe it is you who don't understand, my lord. Whatever you might think you need, I most assuredly do not want. Now leave my house at once and never return."

"Please." He wasn't used to begging. He wasn't too proud to do so, however. Clearing the debt was what mattered. "I know I can't replace what you lost—"

"You'll please refrain from speaking about that which you have no understanding, my lord."

"Just let me pay you. I'll do anything."

That gave her pause. "Anything?"

Cold regret chilled him to the bone. But it was too late—he'd spoken. He wasn't backtracking, not now that he'd broken through the barrier. "Anything."

Her eyes gleamed with malice. "Why don't you come upstairs, my lord? I have an idea that might solve both our problems."

Chapter One

The same afternoon, about an hour later

Lady Elizabeth Rosamund Burke stood at the window, peering down into the street from behind a lapis-blue damask curtain.

Nobody faced down her mother. *Nobody.*

Except this man.

That was to say, he'd tried. If she hadn't overheard the conversation herself, she might have believed him daft, for all he was her dear friend Grace's cousin.

Lord Bennington, the man who had just seen her mother and been told he'd be marrying her ward to pay his debt, was in the street giving a coin to the scrubby boy who'd minded his horse. His expression was intensely savage. Apparently, the conversation had not gone as he'd expected.

Initially he'd refused, of course. And vehemently.

In the end, Lady Rushworth had threatened a suit and finally extracted a reluctant promise that he *would* marry the girl.

A suit meant scandal. If there was anything Eliza had learned about the Landons, it was that living in the dirty wake of the late patriarch's sullied name had driven each and every one to avoid scandal like a prince avoids soot.

With that, her mother had won. The earl had agreed to her terms. He would allow himself to be coerced into marriage.

On the sofa, Eliza's cousin Christiana—her mother's ward—sat weeping quietly. Her spectacles sat in her lap while she dabbed at her eyes with a prettily embroidered handkerchief. "She can't mean to do this to me. She can't. I couldn't bear it."

Eliza turned, hands twisting together in helplessness. They hadn't been meant to hear. It had been a private conversation behind closed doors. But Eliza wasn't sorry they'd listened.

If they hadn't, they wouldn't have learned of Lady Rushworth's plans... Best not to think about that. They knew. And they could prepare.

"We'll think of something."

The words felt hollow. Eliza hadn't the first notion of what it was she might do. But it was imperative she do *something*. Her cousin's life and heart were too important, too dear. She deserved all the chances at love that Eliza could never have for herself.

When he'd been dying, Eliza's father had begged her to take care of Christiana. Eliza had promised.

Seeing how terribly Lady Rushworth treated her made Eliza hurt. For, of course, both of them—Eliza and her mother—knew something about Christiana that Christiana didn't know about herself. She wasn't Eliza's cousin, not really. In truth, they were half sisters. And though it was no fault of Christiana's, Lady Rushworth would never forgive her.

A thousand times Eliza had thought about revealing the sordid facts. A thousand times she'd bitten her tongue.

As she often found herself doing in odd moments,

Eliza searched her companion for any hint of resemblance between them. But she and Christiana could not have been more different. Where she was pale and dark, with straight walnut tresses and ivory skin, Christiana was all wild red curls and vibrant green eyes. Where Eliza's figure and height were average and unassuming, Christiana was short, buxom, unabashedly feminine, and—when her heart wasn't being pounded by her guardian's mallet—bright and sparkling.

Normally, she was full of smiles and good cheer. To see her in so miserable a state tore Eliza's heart in two.

It would do no good to assure the girl that the man didn't appear quite so bad as all that. And not because he was tall and cut a fine figure—the sort one was more likely to read about in certain novels than see for oneself in daily life. The way he'd held his ground, the way he had persisted in the face of certain failure, the way he hadn't answered her mother's vitriol by lashing out in turn…

Two years ago, Christiana had given her heart to a soldier. Tom. They'd loved one another from afar, waiting for her to be of age before they married.

Unfortunately, Lady Rushworth had discovered Christiana's secret correspondence. She'd demanded that Christiana give up the man forever. But Christiana had refused. By marrying her off to Lord Bennington, Lady Rushworth meant to irrevocably part the lovers.

There had to be something Eliza could do to stop this. Her cousin was naught but a few days from her twenty-first birthday. Her prospects couldn't be ruined, not now. Not when she was so close to having everything she wanted.

Lady Rushworth despised the Landons. Despised them with every fiber in her body. Lord Bennington was Jeremy *Landon*, the nephew who'd inherited his wastrel uncle's title, estate, and debts.

True, marrying Christiana to Lord Bennington meant

being connected with the Landons. But, by her mother's logic, it would be far more disgraceful having her niece elope with someone who, as she'd said, *stinks like the commoner he is*.

After overhearing Lady Rushworth's plans for Christiana, their one hope had been that Lord Bennington would refuse the request. He had. Steadfastly. Until Lady Rushworth had threatened him.

Eliza had to do something. She couldn't see her cousin suffer like this. She could not.

But what?

The answer didn't come until a few hours after she'd gone to bed.

Or *an* answer, at any rate. It probably wasn't enough. But to sit idly by and let this happen without trying anything—however desperate—was out of the question.

Eliza lit a candle and silently crept through the house, pausing at her cousin's door to press her ear against the wood panel. No sounds of crying. That was something, at least.

In the sitting room, Eliza sat at the escritoire and withdrew a clean sheet of paper, opened the inkwell, and gently dipped the nib of her pen in the black ink.

She paused, considering how to address him. Was this formal correspondence? Unlikely. It was beyond the pale for her to be writing to a man to whom she was not related.

My lord,

You must not, under any circumstances, marry Lady Rushworth's niece. Doing so would be a terrible mistake.

Frowning, she paused. That wouldn't be enough to convince him to leave off. But what else could she say?

She underlined *not* once. Then again.

Still not enough.

She bent and scratched the pen against the paper some more.

Let me assure you, her heart belongs to another. Call off this scheme at once. A small scandal is nothing compared to two lives being forever ruined. Marrying her ladyship's ward would be the very worst thing you could do for yourself or her. Please, my lord, I beg you—call off this foolishness. Allow her to make the love match she deserves.

There. Now the question was whether or not she should sign her name.

No. Absolutely not.

But then, how could he take assurances from an unnamed person?

It would have to do. To write such a letter at all was an enormous risk. Signing her name would be far too incriminating. Even were she not found out, he would know. A man who'd agree to marry a woman to pay a debt could not be considered trustworthy.

Eliza blotted, folded the sheet, and sealed the note with a wafer.

Back in her bedchamber, she rang the bell.

"Margaret, pray forgive me." Eliza rose when the rumpled face of her sleep-worn maid appeared. "No doubt you've heard what my mother intends for Christiana."

Margaret paused a moment, seemingly unwilling to admit what everyone knew—that the servants gossiped worse than fishwives on a Monday. At last, she muttered something circumspect.

Eliza drew a breath. "What I'm asking of you—well, you have every right to say no to my request, you understand. I will not fault you."

The maid drew herself up, scowling as if suddenly

altogether more alert. She was small of stature, but Lord help the man, woman, or beast who underestimated her. Ferocity, thy name was Margaret. "I'm not afraid of anything, my lady."

Luckily for Eliza, that fierceness extended to Margaret's loyalty to her mistress as well.

"It's the dead of night. Are you sure?"

"I'm not a fool, my lady. I know how to navigate dangers."

"Very good. I need this delivered to Lord Bennington." She handed over the note. "I need it delivered to his hands and nobody else's, and I need assurance that he reads it."

A note like this couldn't be left to languish on a pile of unopened post. Or, worse, be read by someone in the earl's employ.

At her dressing table, Eliza dug through the banknotes in her box of pin money until she found several large coins at the bottom. "One is for you. Spend the rest as you must, to see the task completed. Anything left you may keep."

When Margaret had gone, Eliza slept, but fitfully. Various scenarios of how the earl might react to the letter coiled through her mind again and again, bringing with them sharp turns of emotion. One minute she was certain of success. The next, certain of failure.

By first light, she'd had quite enough and tried to amuse herself with a book.

She jumped at the sound of her door opening. Christiana stood there, her face red and swollen with tears. She sniffed. "I thought you might be awake."

Eliza stood and opened her arms for her cousin. "Come here."

Christiana settled in the embrace, tears flowing freely, soaking the shoulder of Eliza's night rail.

At last, she pulled back and wiped her face. "I won't be able to bear it. I won't. I can't be parted from Tom, I can't. Whenever I think of that horrid old earl..." Her speech dissolved into incomprehensible sounds as crying overtook her once again.

If Eliza had anything to say about it, her cousin wouldn't have to marry "that horrid old earl"—even though to Eliza, who was six and twenty herself, Lord Bennington didn't seem so old.

She dug her teeth into her lip, repeating a silent prayer that her note had reached the man by now—that he'd reconsidered, seen the folly of letting Lady Rushworth control him, and would appear on their doorstep by breakfast to call the whole thing off.

"We'll find a way." Eliza spoke from the depths of her soul. Somehow she would see to it this wedding did *not* happen. "You have my promise. You *won't* marry him."

Christiana shook her head. "Tom and I should run away to Scotland. That's what we should have done in the first place. Or to America."

"No. It won't come to that." Being driven from the lives they led and loved because of one person's distaste for their union didn't seem right. "We'll find a way out—a proper way out."

"How did you endure living when…" Christiana trailed off, giving Eliza a careful look.

There was no question as to what her cousin was referring, though nobody in the house but Lady Rushworth ever dared broach the subject.

Once, a long time ago, Eliza had been engaged. Now it seemed like that life had been lived by someone else and she'd only stood on the side watching. "You mean when I lost Captain Pearson?"

Christiana gave a shy nod.

Oh, but her situation did not compare to her cousin's. Eliza had discovered for herself the foolishness of thinking she could ever be loved by a man.

The burning shame at the remembrance came flooding back, as if the engagement had ended but yesterday.

Used, Captain Pearson had spat before walking out of her life forever. *Ruined. No man is going to want a whore like you.*

In one regard, Eliza was utterly alone—always had been, always would be. She couldn't tell anyone what she'd done. Not again. She'd tried once, with her former beloved, thinking that she owed her future husband the truth about her lack of virginity.

Thank all that was holy she'd told him while they were still merely engaged. If she had told him after they'd married, who knew what misery he might have made her life. The man had a vindictive streak. For her transgression, he might have punished her all the rest of her days.

But she was saved the trouble of having to answer by Margaret's appearance. The maid's significant look sent a jolt through Eliza.

Eliza returned her attention to Christiana. "You return to bed, my dear, and try to sleep."

"There is no way I shall ever be able to sleep again. Not until I know I won't have to marry him."

"I promise you that won't happen."

"But what can you do to prevent it?" Christiana's eyes filled with tears.

"Everything in my power." She prayed she could come up with something to uphold her pledge. "Everything."

Something in Eliza's voice must have assured the girl. That or weariness was finally having the better of her. She gave a halfhearted nod before leaving.

Margaret was scowling. Eliza didn't know what to make of the look. "Well?"

For one breathless moment, Eliza thought Margaret had failed, and her head swirled as though she might have to sit down. But from a hidden pocket in her skirts, the maid withdrew a folded message.

A reply. The paper tore as Eliza ripped the red wax seal.

Matters of the heart have always seemed to me the most foolish consideration in a match.

That was all. No signature. Not even an initial. Nothing.

Eliza wrinkled her nose. She could have sat for a year inventing possible replies to her note, and she would not have come close to considering *this* one.

It took a minute, but it finally dawned on her that she had written about Christiana's heart belonging to another. To *that* was what he'd chosen to reply?

He hadn't said he wasn't going to call off the marriage. But he hadn't said he wouldn't, either. Was she a fool to believe there might be hope?

Before she knew what she was doing, she was back at the escritoire, pen in hand.

You are wrong, my lord. Heartily wrong, and I do not beg your forgiveness in pointing this out to you. Matters of the heart are the most important consideration in marriage.

Poppycock. Eliza might once have believed in matters of the heart. Whether she did or not now, however… The most that could be said was a part of her wanted to believe, if only for her cousin's sake.

The "horrid old earl" need not know her true mind. What mattered was that he did not marry Christiana.

Eliza's heart started beating as her anger went from a simmer to a boil. Who did this man think he was, to agree to such a preposterous notion as paying a debt by taking a bride? Such things weren't done—they simply weren't.

A fierce wave of protectiveness for Christiana washed

over her. She would save her cousin. She *would.*

The tip of Eliza's pen split from the pressure she exerted upon it. It was not so terrible that it needed mending. It only made the lines thicker and darker, which suited her current mood perfectly.

> *But I do not pretend that I will sway your opinion. Indeed, that is not my object in writing to you. Matters of the heart might well be the very last consideration you might have for matrimony. They are, however, the very first consideration of the lady in question. You must respect her feelings. You owe it to both her and yourself to do so. Think of which is the greater honor—clearing out some debt or saving two people from an unwanted marriage? Clearly people matter far more than anything else. If you can't see that, and you force an unwilling woman into marriage, you'll never again be able to call yourself a gentleman. Then you can take your absurd notions of what is honorable all the way to damnation.*

Chapter Two

Call himself a gentleman?

Jeremy was in his library where, for the second time in the last five hours, that strange messenger had called, insisted on seeing nobody but him, and delivered an unsigned note.

He crumpled the paper in his hand and tossed the ball into the empty fireplace. His pulse pounded hard enough to block out every other sound.

How dare this person say such a thing to him? His teeth clenched.

He looked back to the messenger—a small woman of about thirty, with unremarkable features, and a steely look in her narrow, unblinking eyes. "Enough of this absurd game. Tell me who sent this and tell me at once."

"You couldn't pay me enough to say, my lord."

"Is that supposed to be a hint? Is it money you want?"

Her jaw set. There was a long silence.

He put his back to her and pulled out a sheet of paper.

One who hides behind the cowardice of unsigned

notes has little standing where right and honorable behavior is concerned.

Four hours later, the messenger returned a third time. Jeremy sighed, pushed his empty coffee cup away, and opened his hand to receive the note.

You compare unsigned notes to marrying a woman who would rather see herself dead than be your bride? Have you no heart?

The question required but a single word.

No.

Business took Jeremy out for the remainder of the day—business being going to the Doctors' Commons to see the archbishop about a special license. The trip illuminated one critical oversight: he didn't know the name of his bride.

The clerk met the revelation with incredulous surprise. "Don't know the name of the lady to whom you're about to be married?"

For the first time in memory, Jeremy was speechless. He'd been so rattled by being forced into agreeing to marry to clear the debt, he'd never asked—and hadn't realized his oversight until standing there attempting to apply for a special license. He could ill afford such slips. For one thing, he didn't want anyone to have any ability to rattle him. Least of all, Lady Rushworth. More importantly, if he began making mistakes in smaller matters, what would stop him from making mistakes in more important ones?

The clerk tutted, peering over his spectacles at Jeremy. "Most irregular, my lord. Most irregular. Did you think we didn't have to verify that you were both eligible to wed before the license could be issued?"

Later that day, without having procured the license, he

indulged in a ride through the park at the fashionable hour. The uncomfortable incident with the clerk still stung his pride, so the choice might not have been the best. As much as he loved riding his horse, Poseidon, walking the beast through crowds of people was not helping to relax him. Since inheriting the title, he'd come to know very few of them. Almost none, in fact. And the odd squints he received—like people couldn't quite place him—were proof enough of that.

Jeremy had little use for Society. He'd spent ten years absorbed in nothing but the tangled affairs of the estate, having had but a few months between the end of his schooling and his uncle's death. His birth and station placed him firmly among these people. The stain of his uncle's scandal placed him outside them all, regardless of his title.

He wasn't certain he cared.

The scandal rankled, that was true. To be so harshly judged by the actions of another…they were small concerns. Petty. Why people buried their heads in such matters when the country was at war, while a mad king sat on the throne, while the American president had put an embargo on trade relations, and the prime minister had been outright murdered just outside the House of Commons…

Jeremy's grip on the reins tightened. Poseidon was a dark bay stallion, highly trained and sensitive to the slightest change in his rider, and the creature stopped at Jeremy's slight movement. He relaxed his hands back into a proper position for holding the leathers and urged the horse forward.

As much as he wanted to put the problem aside for the afternoon, the thoughts of his impending marriage, his pride, and those letters wouldn't fully dissolve from his mind.

Those letters. Those letters. Every female face made him wonder—was that the woman who'd been sending him the unsigned notes?

The truth was, he needed to see who would write in

passionate defense of someone she loved. All the talk of hearts and love matches aside, he admired her boldness.

Returning from the rather dull turn of the park, Jeremy handed his things over to the butler, a thin-haired man who muttered complaints about rheumatism when he thought others couldn't overhear. "Did that little messenger return while I was out, Templeton?"

"No, my lord."

Perhaps the plague of unwanted notes had come to an end.

Which didn't solve the problem of the restlessness in Jeremy's bones. He wanted to prowl London and hunt for the woman who'd penned those words to him.

He shouldn't have been unsettled. He knew his own mind well enough. As an earl, he'd long been reconciled to the fact that one day he'd marry. When he did, he was under no delusion of undertaking the obligation for any reasons but the most practical.

Marrying to pay a debt had never occurred to him, but it would do as well as anything else.

And yet, that talk of hearts and love…he wanted to rebel against the wrongness of it.

Tomorrow he would do what he should have done in the beginning. He'd have the messenger followed.

Later that night, Jeremy was in his bath when Templeton appeared. Nobody interrupted Jeremy's bath—not ever.

He knew at once why the servant dared to break the rule. "Another note?"

"Forgive me for the intrusion, my lord, but I thought you would want to see it immediately."

He sat up, steaming water rippling around him. "I'm

surprised the messenger allowed it to be taken by anybody but me."

"She clearly struggled with herself before doing so. However, she seemed less keen on seeing you in your bath than on not delivering the message."

"She's waiting?" Jeremy, wiping his wet hands on the nearby linen, took the note from the silver tray Templeton held and slid his finger under the asymmetrical globule of sealing wax.

"Indeed, my lord."

Jeremy scanned his eyes over the words.

My mistake, my lord, in thinking you might have a heart. It's perfectly clear to me now that one who would agree to such a dastardly scheme, who would marry a woman he knows to be unwilling, could not possibly possess one, and I am left only to be ashamed of myself for having not seen as much sooner.

Since you have admitted your deficit, let me instead act on your reason—you are possessed of reason, are you not?

I'll proceed as if the answer is yes.

Marrying an unwilling woman is barbaric. This is the nineteenth century. You are not a knight bound by oath to a tyrannical queen. You are an earl. Not an earl in the highest standing, true, but that is no fault of yours.

Knowing what I do of your family—and it's more than you might think, more than perhaps you yourself know—you want nothing to do with even the slightest hint of scandal.

What you also don't know, or perhaps, don't want

to admit, is that the situation you're walking into has the rank odor of scandal emanating from it. If you're going to be a selfish clod concerned solely with yourself, you'd best consider what it will mean when people find out what you've done to this poor woman.

And they will find out. I'll publish far and wide. Just consider—soon you'll be known across the kingdom as having done the unthinkable. Nobody could believe you capable of upstaging your late uncle. You think you're disgraced now. You wait. You're about to prove them all wrong.

Threats? The writer must have been feeling the helplessness of her situation. It was almost enough to make him feel sorry for her. Whoever she was.

He rose and, without drying himself off, walked fully nude across the room to pen his reply.

But that business about doing something worse than his uncle made his teeth set.

Name yourself at once.

He handed the sealed paper to his waiting butler.

"Have the messenger followed, will you?" Because he didn't expect the writer to admit her identity. "I want to discover who she's working for, once and for all."

The answer wasn't long in returning. When it came he was freshly bathed, in his banyan, settled in a chair by the fire with a book.

"The messenger returned to Lady Rushworth's home, my lord."

Ah. So the notes must be coming from his future bride. Of course. The simplest answer was usually correct. He should have guessed sooner.

As it happened, after gaining the intelligence, another note didn't take long to appear. True to his assumption—which he might have admired under different circumstances—she didn't reveal her name.

Your heart and conscience.

Was her assurance little more than bluster and bravado? Did she feel safe in believing herself anonymous? Or was she really so spirited?

When the note arrived about her heart belonging to another, he'd pictured a woman collapsed in a heap of tears. But going back over what she'd written—including the one he'd crumpled, having been rescued from the unused fireplace before a servant might be overcome with curiosity—there didn't appear to be any tearstains on the paper.

Late into the night, one line in particular continued to bother Jeremy. It wasn't that business about hearts and consciences. It was the line about knowing his family as she did.

Which brought him to his cousin's house at breakfast time the next day.

Grace—Lady Corbeau as of the first of the new year—rose to greet him when he arrived. But her wide smile faded when he couldn't return the warmth. She was alone in the small room, the walls of which were the color of robin's eggs.

"Is something wrong? Here. Sit." She gestured to a seat. "I'll fix you a plate and have some coffee made."

"Thank you, cousin."

It wasn't until smelling the foods laden on the side table did he realize that he had taken nothing this morning. Against all odds, his appetite hadn't faltered, his stomach growling to remind its owner that Jeremy lived to serve it—not the other way around.

She put a full plate in front of him. Hardly seeing what he

consumed, he dived in.

"Something is the matter, isn't it?" Grace was the eldest of the four daughters of the old earl. Her next sister, Isabel, was Jeremy's mother's companion—among other things he didn't presently care to contemplate—while Jane was off he wasn't certain where, and Phoebe had recently married, making a rather surprising choice for her husband.

"Haven't you heard?" He washed down a bite with a swallow of perfectly brewed coffee. It was rich and smooth and strong. "I'm to be married."

Her eyes went wide. So she hadn't heard. Interesting.

"Married? To whom? I didn't know you had anyone in mind who you thought might suit you. When did this happen?"

Jeremy and Grace were becoming reacquainted—and only just—but there'd been a quick rapport between them. No sooner had he returned to London than she'd made an overture of friendship to end the estrangement between the two branches of the family.

It was the last thing he himself had considered doing, connecting with his family—other than his mother and brother, of course—but Grace hadn't had to persist long.

She possessed all the exact qualities he most valued in a friend. She was an easy person with whom to talk, forthright and frank without being harsh or off-putting. She gave him the sense that she never judged others but instead tried to understand their point of view—without excusing bad behavior.

If he'd known that he would like her so very much, he'd have sought a reconciliation himself, and much sooner than she had.

"The day before yesterday. And I didn't have anyone in mind. The whole thing was thrust upon me, most unwillingly."

Grace raised her brows. "When it comes to marriage, cousin, few people can be truly forced. And even then, the circumstances have to be fairly extreme, and they still have to say yes. Is this a matter of honor or urgency?"

"No. Nothing like that."

"I thought not."

"It's the debt—the one I told you about."

"Oh, the last debt. The one Lady Rushworth is refusing to accept." Grace's mouth pursed as she considered. "But how does the debt figure into marriage?"

"I foolishly told her I'd do anything. She held me at my word."

His cousin grimaced. "I don't think I understand. You can't mean you're marrying Lady Rushworth."

"Good God, no." Jeremy downed the rest of his coffee in one swallow as if it were tonic against the horrifying notion. "Nothing like that. She's decided that in order to consider the debt cleared, I must marry her *ward*."

Grace's jaw went slack. "Lady Rushworth's niece? You can't be serious."

"I wish I weren't."

"I've never heard of such a thing."

"She's manipulating me."

Grace's color rose. She went indignant. "What does the poor girl who's being made to marry you—what does *she* have to say about this…this absurdity?"

Jeremy couldn't reveal their correspondence. Doing so would have felt like betraying a confidence. Unrelated men and women were not supposed to exchange letters. He didn't care for lying, either, but it was the lesser of two sins. "I don't know."

"You don't know? Oughtn't you to find out?"

"I have a runner friend in Bow Street. I sent a message this morning asking him to find out what he can for me about Lady Rushworth's ward."

"That's *not* what I mean, and you know it. You can't

possibly go through with this. It's not right."

"Marriages have begun on less provocation than the payment of a debt."

"Is that supposed to excuse your behavior?"

"No, I suppose not."

She gave a nod. "You can't possibly expect happiness from this arrangement."

"I don't expect happiness in marriage one way or the other. That's not the point, is it?"

Grace took a long breath and scowled into her tea, brow furrowed as she remained lost in thought for a terse moment.

Finally, she spoke again. "But Lady Rushworth despises the Landons. She can't possibly want her niece to *marry* one of us. It's hard enough on the poor woman that I married her godson."

"Yes, well, the poor woman, as you say, threatened to sue me over the debt if I didn't go along with her scheme."

"How can she sue you? You're making reparations."

"But the original debt wasn't money. Her husband loaned your father a jewel. You don't happen to know anything about that, do you?"

"A jewel? No, I've never heard of anything like it. It sounds a bit odd, to say the truth." She sighed, head tilting a bit to the side. "But I'm afraid I know little about anything my father did, other than what people care to tell me—and I take pleasure in knowing that while what they say might contain a grain of fact, it's most likely fabricated."

"Unless I can produce the jewel, she says I must marry her ward. I've been searching for it for years. It's long gone."

That damn jewel. Jeremy had hired runners to track it down, but it had vanished without a trace. It didn't help that nobody knew what sort of jewel for which they were supposed to have been looking. He'd gone back to those scraps of paper he'd pieced together again and again to see if he'd imagined it. The handwriting wasn't clear, but it was the only thing he'd been able to make of it. The late Lord Rushworth had loaned Jeremy's uncle a jewel. Lady Rushworth hadn't denied it.

"What could she possibly gain from a suit? You can't conjure the jewel from nothing, and you've proven that you're more than willing to make reparations."

"She wants to stir up old scandals, don't you see?"

"Well, you're not going along with such nonsense, are you?"

"What other choice do I have?"

"Every choice in the world. Say no. Don't let the old harridan bully you into something so utterly absurd. I happen to know Lady Rushworth's daughter quite well, and I've come to know the ward a little as well. You and she wouldn't suit."

"It's a marriage. All I require is an upstanding, reasonably highborn woman completely free of scandal to see my duty to the line complete."

"Heirs, you mean."

"Yes."

Grace *tsked* and shook her head, raising her gaze to the ceiling. "Listen to yourself."

Chapter Three

Normally, today would have been Lady Rushworth's day out. And of course, because it wasn't the day she was at home to accept calls, nobody paid any.

The hours of the day hung all but stagnant. The three of them sat together in the drawing room. Alone. In stifling silence.

Except for the pounding of Eliza's heart. Really, that the pace and force of the beats hadn't caught her mother's attention yet could be nothing but a small miracle.

Christiana was pale, with hollow eyes, her head bowed to a meek angle. Lady Rushworth—well, she was as she always was.

Eliza attempted to work on her embroidery. Her hands trembled so hard, she kept having to pick out stitches.

"Oh!" She brought her finger, sharp with bright pain, to her mouth, but not before smearing the white field of her fabric canvas with bright blood.

Christiana started and peered over anxiously, her spectacles sliding down her nose. "What happened?"

"I pricked myself."

Lady Rushworth's brows sank, and she shook her head. "Have care, Eliza."

The metallic bite of blood filled Eliza's mouth. The frustration of the pain caused by her own carelessness made her bold. "Mother, you can't make Christiana marry Lord Bennington."

Both of them looked at her in surprise, the resulting silence seeming to conspire against her with malicious intent. Christiana blanched while Lady Rushworth's countenance reddened.

"She *will* marry him. There is nothing more to discuss. The day after tomorrow, at precisely eleven o'clock, she will become Lady Bennington."

Eliza's insides burned with rage. She'd spent years enduring her mother's selfish whims and her contempt for others. When Eliza's father was alive, they'd had one another. Then, without warning, he'd died. Until the morning they'd found him cold and gray, he'd been in the best of health.

If her mother pushed her cousin into this absurd marriage, Christiana would be lonely and forlorn. Having spent so many years alone after her father's death, Eliza knew all too well what it was to be imprisoned in isolation. She wouldn't wish that on anybody. Least of all, Christiana.

Eliza glanced to her cousin, willing all the strength and determination now surging through her veins to take root in Christiana as well. But Christiana hung her head, hiding her trembling lip, no doubt. All her vibrancy had been sapped away by Lady Rushworth's machinations.

"You can't make her say yes, Mother." Eliza would be strong for them both. She threw her shoulders back. "All she has to do is say no loudly and clearly."

Lady Rushworth's features went cold. She spoke with the certainty of one used to holding power over the weak. "She *will* say yes."

Awash in helpless frustration, Eliza gnashed her teeth. There was going to be a way out of this. And it would *not* involve running away to the next ship leaving Newport for America or India or some other horribly distant place.

Even if they had the means, fleeing would be allowing her mother to win, in a sense, by forcing them from their homes and lives. They shouldn't have to forfeit so much simply to escape a bad marriage.

The trouble was, at the moment, there were no other options on the table.

"This came for you, my lady." Margaret plucked a small note from the side of the tray on which she carried a pot of chocolate. "I almost didn't intercept it before Caruthers delivered it to your mother."

Eliza sat up in bed, hands shaking so hard she almost couldn't read the latest note from the earl.

> *I know you're my intended, and I hope by now you've come to accept your fate, as I have. Send along your name so I might have it for the special license. We can be married as early as tomorrow and have this whole business over with once and for all. Don't bother with fripperies. Dress for travel. I don't care much for London. After the ceremony, we shall set out at once for Idlewood.*

His intended?

Chocolate forgotten on the side table, Eliza wore nothing but a shift as she took her place at the writing desk she'd had brought up to her room and placed on the table by the window. The room was cool in the clean early-morning light.

Carefully, she dipped the pen, and drew a deep breath. The nib slid smoothly over the paper, leaving a shining black trail after it as she formed the stroke and curve of each letter.

Elizabeth Rosamund Burke

Her stomach sank into an abyss. She should burn the paper. Immediately. She couldn't take Christiana's place as Lord Bennington's bride. What an absurd notion.

But another part of her wanted to do exactly that. It would serve the heartless louse right, wouldn't it?

And once he married her, marrying Christiana would be quite impossible.

Eliza bit her lip. Could she marry a stranger? She knew nothing about the man. Nothing real, that was.

According to her mother, all Landons were cheats and liars, and Lady Rushworth held up Eliza's friend Grace as the prime example. Grace had been forced into an engagement with Lord Corbeau, her mother's beloved godson. Lady Rushworth had never believed that Grace hadn't contrived to be caught in that storeroom with her now husband—her beloved husband, at that—and Eliza had eventually given up trying to convince her otherwise.

If Eliza herself married a Landon—became a Landon—her mother would never forgive her. But if her mother forced Christiana to marry Lord Bennington, Eliza would never forgive her mother.

Once, a very long time ago, Eliza had taken for granted that she would marry. It was what women of her class did. When she'd become engaged to Captain Pearson, her mother had been overjoyed.

What a dark day it had been when she'd had to break the news to Lady Rushworth that the engagement had been broken. After absorbing the shock, all her mother's hopes for her had been lost.

Since then, Eliza had known she was fated for eternal spinsterhood. At first, she'd mourned what she'd lost. Eventually, she'd accepted it. In time, she'd come to like the idea of remaining single forever.

Or she thought she had. Unexpectedly, the idea of leaving her mother once and for all made her almost dizzy with longing. She had money. Lots of money. None of which she could touch. It was all for her dowry. There had never been any doubt in her late father's mind that his beautiful and beloved daughter would marry and marry well. So, of course, there had been no need to make her independent.

Indeed, she had almost fulfilled all their assumptions. Captain Pearson had been the dashing naval hero with whom the whole of England had fallen in love. And he'd wanted her. Until the fateful night she'd told him the truth.

What would her father say if he knew what she was planning now?

"Margaret?" Eliza turned to where her maid was choosing her mistress's morning gown.

"Yes, my lady?"

"We need all our things packed by tonight. Christiana's, too. But you must do so in secret. It's absolutely essential that nobody else in the house learn of what you're doing. Is that understood?" Her pulse pounded with such bestial severity, she could hardly hear herself. Her voice sounded strange—and very far away. She couldn't do this. She couldn't. The plan would be found out immediately. It had to be. It was too absurd to possibly work.

"My lady, I…" Margaret's mouth remained open as her words trailed away.

Eliza stood on shaky legs. "I have every faith that you can manage the task beautifully."

Sometimes it was better to display more confidence than one actually felt. In the next thirty or so hours, she'd have to maintain the guise.

And if she were found out?

She'd deal with the aftermath when it became necessary. She'd never faced down her mother for a transgression of this magnitude before. Whether she was successful or whether she was not, one way or the other, she would be answering for her actions.

• • •

Eliza had endured a guilty conscience before. Losing her virginity at fourteen, then having nobody in whom to confide when the full magnitude of her horrendous mistake had come crashing down. Knowing she'd been completely at fault and having to live alone and isolated with her shame pressing down upon her.

Then, later, losing Captain Pearson.

At least he'd never betrayed her secret to Society at large. He could have taken vengeance upon her by exposing her for the ruined woman she was. His anger had frightened her, and she'd spent a year sick with worry that her world was on the verge of collapsing.

It was very much the same feeling now as a butler brought Eliza and her cousin into the earl's foyer. Any moment, her mother would burst through the door, and there was going to be hell to pay.

"Miss Elizabeth Burke, I assume?" As she handed over her things to the butler, Eliza turned to the deep voice. She opened her mouth to answer, but the sight of the man—a stranger—made language shrivel up, lost and forgotten against the realization that she meant to deceive him at the altar. "You're early. Where's Lady Rushworth?"

From a distance, the earl had been perfectly admirable. Straight and tall, with the wide berth of his shoulders set off against the lean taper of his waist and long legs.

Up close he was...arresting. She took the measure of the man she was going to trick into marriage. He had distinctive features cut of hard angles—terribly handsome and brutally masculine. But it was the brilliant aquamarine irises that all but did her in. The strength of his gaze nearly suspended the frantic beating of her heart. Lord save her. What would he do when he discovered he'd married Lady Rushworth's daughter instead of her ward?

It wasn't right, what Eliza was doing. But at least *she* was going into the union willingly.

She was so close, but everything could still go horribly wrong.

By her side, Christiana cowered, looking as if she were trying to make herself small and insignificant. Her face paled to an unnatural color, and she kept her head bowed, even as Eliza presented her to the earl.

"Lady Rushworth"—Eliza had to be extremely careful not to call the woman her mother as she sidestepped the question of their early arrival—"chose not to come."

"You're in luck. The good reverend came sooner than expected, too. I suppose we might as well get this thing done with."

She prickled. Get it done with, indeed. "Is the eradication of the debt so important that you're going to insist upon going through with this absurd scheme?"

The man's mouth flattened into a critical line. "Forgive me for being unable to give you the answer you want. But you have never been in debt. You don't know what it's like to be shadowed by the sins of another."

Eliza couldn't answer, but not for the reason the earl might suppose. No, she'd not been shadowed by the sins of another. She'd been shadowed by sins of her own—sins far more dire than debt.

Was there any way she might escape her new husband finding out about what she'd done? He expected a virgin, no doubt. As had Captain Pearson. Unlike the captain, the earl wouldn't be able to toss her aside and end the engagement. No, they'd be married.

She wouldn't let her mind wander through that territory—not now. There were too many things to think about, too many implications of her deception to struggle against. What did they matter? She was doing this to save Christiana.

While the earl directed the servants to begin loading their trunks onto his coach, Eliza slipped her hand into her cousin's and squeezed. It was as much for Christiana as to give herself courage. It was happening. She was about to fool a man into marrying her. And she would forever be in a kind of debt of her own for the consequences of her actions.

Chapter Four

Jeremy prided himself on control. On keeping a cool, level head, no matter what life might throw at him.

He couldn't stop glancing at the figure who stood beside him as they spoke their marriage vows in his parlor. Women had taken his breath away before. But the first glance at the woman who was to be his wife had made his jaw slacken and his mouth go dry. She utterly redefined his notions of beauty.

She was fixed with the refined elegance of complicated details that worked together to form a pleasingly simple whole. Her face was more square than oval, but the deviation from fashion heightened her allure rather than detracted from it. Because he was so close, he could see minute details—the wide hazel eyes were golden brown around the pupil and moved to blue green at the edge of her iris.

And that dark hair…oh, that dark hair. If she knew what it inspired in him, she might not appear so outwardly calm.

Jeremy's mind wandered back to the notes they'd exchanged, which drew his gaze back to her yet again. There was fire under that elegant exterior, which intensified his curiosity to unwrap the pretty package.

In more ways than one.

There was the business of heirs to be seen to, and why not beget children with a woman who stirred his blood? This was not the time or the place, however, to be thinking about *that*. Hell, it wasn't even an appropriate time to be having the revelation.

He'd had little more than a handful of days to become accustomed to the idea that the choice of wife had been stolen from him. Lady Rushworth was the last person he would have wanted to force a bride upon him.

He'd struggled with himself since that fateful meeting. Was he going to allow her to manipulate him? Apparently so, because just then, as he refocused his attention on the business at hand, the clergyman pronounced them man and wife.

It was done. The final debt was paid, now and forever.

They'd met for the first time not a quarter of an hour ago. They were strangers to one another. And they were bound together for the rest of their lives.

His new wife had turned ashen. The cousin she'd brought with her stood behind them looking shocked. They glanced at one another in silent communication. Saying what, though, he couldn't have guessed. It was as if they couldn't believe what had happened.

Jeremy's brother, Arthur, appeared perfectly disinterested as he went to the sideboard and poured himself a drink. Their mother was in Bath but hadn't been able to make the trip quickly enough, and so had to forgo the attempt.

So he'd had to make do with Arthur as a witness. Whatever Arthur's motive for coming, it almost assuredly did not include familial duty. He turned up exclusively when he needed money—money he believed he could wheedle from Jeremy. Unfortunately for him, Jeremy wasn't about to hand over so much as a ha'penny. If he had, it would be lost over cards before nightfall.

Arthur came to stand by Jeremy's side, watching Eliza from a distance with an unblinking stare. "I'd wager a good deal of money that nobody in London has seen a bride less pleased than yours is now."

Jeremy's teeth clenched at the word "wager."

"There are few things I despise more than gambling."

Scandal, maybe, but so long as Arthur stayed clear of childish antics, there was nothing in Jeremy's life that would drag him into public humiliation.

"And few things I love more." The focus of Arthur's attention hadn't moved. "I must say, she's far more becoming than I expected her to be."

The subject of his new wife's beauty wasn't a topic he'd discuss with his brother. From a sidelong glance, Jeremy caught his bride holding out her hand to study the ring on her finger. She wasn't admiring it. It appeared more like she was puzzling over it.

The scene—and his having surreptitiously caught sight of it—pulled on his insides in an odd way he couldn't name.

"I was surprised when I heard you'd be married secretly." Arthur sipped the wine, seeming not to notice Jeremy's reticence. Or, equally likely, not caring. "It's terribly out of character for you. As close to scandal as you'll ever come, I daresay. But then I thought, it's about time you did something to upset the order you so love and live up to the Landon name."

Inwardly, Jeremy bridled at the suggestion he might do anything scandalous. With his family's history, he could afford no mistakes. "It wasn't secret. I told Mother. And you."

Telling his brother might have been the result of fanciful thinking. They weren't close. He knew Arthur's ways. It had seemed necessary for a family member to be present at the occasion. In retrospect, he should have given the impulse more thought.

"Ah, that might have been what you did, but that won't be the perception. And perception"—he gave Jeremy a sly glance—"is everything."

"That's true only if one believes it to be true. And I, for one, don't believe that for a second."

Arthur burst into laughter. "You care more about perception than anybody I've ever known."

His brother was baiting him, and he would not rise to the call. Neither, however, could he allow the comment to go unremarked. "I know exactly on which point you're confused. What you're mistaking for my caring about *perception* is actually my caring for the history and legacy of our family, for the people who rely on Idlewood for their livelihood, and for a basic level of integrity and morality—"

"Do you bluster on so in Parliament, too, brother? I daresay I should have you in my bedchamber to blather on in just such a manner on nights I can't sleep."

Determined not to let Arthur have the better of him, Jeremy left his brother and went to take his new wife's arm. At her nearness, his blood warmed. She smelled ever so faintly of roses. The light fragrance made him want to step closer. To bend his head and trace the line of her neck as he inhaled the scent of her skin.

He fought against the sensation. It did not bode well to be so easily provoked. Then again, maybe it did. Was pleasure in the company of a beautiful woman a thing to scorn? So long as he could maintain control of himself—and he always did, so he had no reason to worry—he would be safe enough.

"May I call you Elizabeth?" he asked gently.

Her color heightened. Perhaps their closeness did to her what it also did to him? "Nobody calls me Elizabeth. I prefer Eliza."

Eliza. Simple, yet elegant. Like her.

"It's perfect." The words came out lower than he'd anticipated, and much more velvety. Almost as though he was keen to seduce her.

Hell, he might be.

He'd given up quite a lot when he'd become the Earl of Bennington. Like music. Once he'd played the violin. But he was unlikely to ever pick one up again, even if every time it crossed his mind, his fingers flexed and curled to feel the instrument again.

"We'll be getting an early start. I don't care for London much, I'm afraid, and I plan to spend little time here." He'd already seen his man of business. He paid well to see all his affairs were handled so he could avoid town entirely. "We might as well take advantage of the extra time and leave as soon as possible. We have a long day of travel ahead of us. You're not hungry, are you?"

"No, my lord."

His mind returned to the notes they'd exchanged. She'd said her heart belonged to another. When he'd read her admission, he hadn't much cared. The note from his friend the runner who'd looked into Lady Rushworth's ward had mentioned a soldier she loved. Jeremy had shrugged.

He was sorry to cause anyone pain, yes, but love matches were absurd. There was no guarantee of happiness. His parents had been in love when they'd married. Look what had happened to them. So much anger. So many tears. So many nights he'd found his mother hunched over her dressing table weeping. His mother's heartbreak. His father's cold bitterness.

Or worse—his uncle and aunt. His aunt claimed she'd loved the reckless debtor to the end. But the man's vice had ruined his family. He had ruined all of them, including his daughters, and that was a sin Jeremy could not forgive. Women depended on men, and it was the duty of the stronger sex to protect and care for the weaker.

Love was nothing but a dangerous delusion.

Now that he himself was married, he would fulfill his duties to his wife. No matter how they'd come together, the fact of the matter was, they were linked, perhaps for the remainder of eternity.

Why had Lady Rushworth been so insistent that he marry this woman? She had her own reasons, no doubt. Nefarious and vile. He might never know. It was probably better that way.

A horrible possibility struck him. What if she and the man she'd loved had found a way to be together and she was with child?

How did a man ask such a thing of his new wife? *My dear, you don't happen to be carrying your lover's child, do you?* And what was she supposed to do if she were? Admit the truth?

"We'll spend most of the day on the road, I'm afraid, but we'll reach Idlewood by about midday tomorrow." He cast a glance at Eliza's cousin, who was still so pale and silent. The girl wouldn't look at him. Did he frighten her? She was dressed for travel as well. "Am I to understand your cousin will be accompanying us?"

"Indeed, my lord."

"Very good." At the back of his mind lingered the knowledge that someone else might be accompanying them as well—the man whose name and memory his wife carried in her heart. Jeremy didn't care. He *wouldn't* care. "I'm pleased you'll have a companion."

And all the more pleased he had an excuse to ride alongside the carriage instead of inside with her. With that in mind, he ordered a horse be saddled. When it was ready, the three descended from the house into the street. He helped his wife's companion into the carriage first and was about to help Eliza.

When she took his hand, she glanced at him as if she hadn't anticipated his touch. Their eyes met, and they lingered together a moment in the late morning light. An awareness rushed through his blood, warm and strangely—for all his previous dalliances—unfamiliar. Neither spoke.

Did she feel the current? Was it running between them? Or did it affect only him…perhaps it was his lascivious side rearing its ugly head in an inappropriate time and place.

Her gaze dropped, and her cheeks bloomed a rosy pink. Her reaction sent a surge of satisfaction through him. Oh, yes. She felt it, too.

When her mouth opened as if she sought something to say, he couldn't help himself. He bent. He brushed his lips against hers. They barely touched, but the heat that seared his skin could have made him forget they were in the street where anyone could see them. A jeering tradesman passing with his mule and cart broke the spell.

Eliza started, looking away. Jeremy cleared his throat and helped her the rest of the way into the carriage. When he latched the door shut, his mood soured. By her own account, she'd given her heart to another. He'd told himself he didn't care. That it didn't matter because love in marriage was fit only for poets and fools. But he had to admit that being near her and thinking about her loving someone else stirred jealousy he'd believed himself incapable of feeling. He didn't want to ponder the fact that she loved a man not himself.

And in light of this uncomfortable knowledge, riding horseback to Idlewood was all the more welcome. It was best to put distance between himself and his beautiful new bride.

• • •

"Are you still awake?" Christiana whispered in the small

room at the inn where she and Eliza shared the single narrow bed.

Margaret slept on a pallet and snored softly. The earl had taken his own room.

"Yes." Eliza was staring at the ceiling. Sleep would be difficult to come by tonight. She was married. There was a gold band on her finger to prove as much. It felt heavy—almost a burden on her conscience, knowing the earl had put the ring on the wrong woman.

Christiana pulled the blanket higher. "What are you going to do when he finds out?"

They'd spent all day in the carriage together, neither of them daring to speak of Eliza's deception. It didn't seem real.

Maybe some things were easier to acknowledge in the dark.

"I don't know." If only Eliza had a ready answer. What would she do? "Except he can't find out, can he? Not from another person. I must tell him myself."

For all Christiana knew, they were talking about the marriage. Nothing else. Eliza, however, was also talking about her greatest sin: she'd lain with a man not her husband.

She and her cousin were wrapped in blackness, but still Eliza had to squeeze her eyes shut as she struggled against an onslaught of painful memories. If she could but speak to her younger self—explain everything to her. Tell her what choice would cost her. Marriage to the captain. Happiness.

And now she'd tricked an earl into marrying her. An earl who believed her to be a virgin and Lady Rushworth's ward. Her mistake was going to cost her. Again. It was worse than having married the wrong woman. He'd married a *ruined* woman.

Yet, she closed her eyes and feathered the tips of her fingers over her lips. The kiss they'd shared outside the carriage hadn't been much of anything. She'd gotten and received more affection from cats.

The earl, however, was a far cry from a cat. The nearness of him had made her shiver. And when his skin had brushed against hers, she'd gone warm in thoroughly indecent places. It would have been welcome were there not these secrets between them.

"Do you think…" Christiana's voice wavered. "Do you think I should have given up Tom and married Lord Bennington myself?"

"What?" Eliza grabbed her cousin's hand, squeezing it reassuringly. "No. I do not think that. Not at all."

"It seems so unspeakably selfish. What you did—"

"I did it because I wanted to do it. I wanted to preserve your chance at happiness."

"But what about yours? Now you'll never be able to find love."

Eliza was silent. "Love isn't what everyone wants in a marriage." Once it had been what Eliza wanted. Not anymore.

"I'm willing to believe that." Christiana's voice went to a low whisper. "But what you did—"

"*Shh*. It's done. There is no use thinking about what else we might have attempted."

"I can never repay you."

Eliza started. "Repay me? Banish the thought from your mind this instant. I expect only one thing in return—that you choose your own husband wisely."

"There will never be anybody for me but Tom."

After losing Captain Pearson, Eliza had worked for years to accept that she wasn't destined for love. Not a romantic love, the kind her friend Grace had found, or the kind to which Christiana clung.

At last she knew why. Fate had saved her to be able to help Christiana instead. It was a different kind of love. Her role was as an instrument. Not as a vessel.

But that was one more secret to keep. One more item in her collection she tended alone, protecting those she loved from awful truths.

She'd thought she'd long put away those childish sentiments. Marrying the earl today had brought old heartaches to the surface.

"Then in all the ways that matter, I did the right thing."

She prayed she'd remain so certain of her convictions when the time came to confess to her husband.

Chapter Five

By rights, Jeremy's new wife should have been with him. Not next door with her companion and maid. It would be damned hard to wait—a point on which the erection straining at his falls agreed—but Jeremy was determined not to take her to bed until they reached Idlewood. An inn was no place for a wedding night.

Besides, he had a history of certain behavior at inns, a history which he was not keen to be haunted by when the time came to consummate his marriage. There was a reason he never traveled from home without half a dozen packets of sheaths.

In truth, he stung with shame for all those times he had set aside what was right and given in to his very worst self—that was to say, when he'd bought a dark-haired wench for the simple price of a few coins. It had been transactional. Pleasure for gold. Nothing simpler.

Or so he had told himself.

After that all-too-chaste kiss that had been anything but innocent, it seemed vile to think he ever could have succumbed to such abhorrent behavior. It seemed disloyal to Eliza. His *wife*.

True, she hadn't been his wife then. But she was now, and he was a stronger man than that. He could have kept his so-called needs in check. In retrospect, he'd fed himself lies as a poor excuse for a break in morality.

But it was still difficult to retire alone tonight. Was his wife on the other side of the wall fretting as to why he hadn't wanted to visit her bed tonight? Perhaps he should have explained himself so as to avoid the risk of offending her.

Or perhaps she was relieved, believing that he'd married her but had no intention of ever coming to her bed.

No, she'd know he needed an heir.

Jeremy checked the lock on his door and went to sit on his own bed. He took out a handkerchief and undid his falls, freeing his erection at long last. He might not have his wife to make love to, but if he didn't take matters in hand, so to speak, he'd be in danger of going mad before they reached Idlewood.

Grasping himself, he began to stroke—slowly at first, imagining what it would be like to take off his wife's clothing one piece at a time. He was ready to go and could have had himself off in a second. But it would have been bad form. It was going to be difficult enough restraining himself the first time they were pressed against one another, bare skin against bare skin, as he worked himself inside her.

Imagined scenes of them together spun through his mind. Eliza's dark hair down about her shoulders. His lips plying kisses upon the length of her neck. His wife's breathy moans as he used his fingers to pleasure her—*Oh!*

In a hard burst of powerful throbs, he came…all over his hand.

Bloody nuisance, that.

...

Jeremy never tired of the moment when Idlewood came into view. The house rose from the land, stately and serene amid the wild countryside she inhabited. He inhaled the scents of fresh earth and new greenery. They had to travel a fair bit of the estate before the house itself became visible from the road. The downy world, lush with springtime, split to reveal her hidden secrets. Only wait until he could explore Eliza and revel in her beauty the same way.

When he'd first arrived at the place, it had been neglected and overrun. Fields worked past capacity, the house emptied of anything of value and left to fall to ruin.

That had been his legacy. But by God, it would not be the legacy for the next generation.

Years of doing nothing but rebuilding and restoring had brought Idlewood back from certain destruction. He'd lured tenants back with new cottages—for which he'd had to take on more debt than he would have liked—and exceptionally good terms for rent.

It was paying off beautifully. The chances he'd taken, his tenacity, and his abject refusal to give up. The land was healing, returning from fallow neglect to bountiful fertility.

Today, sitting tall on horseback next to the carriage in which his wife rode—today was the first day real pride swelled to fill Jeremy's chest. She represented a new beginning, too. For the family. For the estate. For himself.

He'd run through a dozen different scenarios to welcome his new bride home. Most of them involved emptying the house of servants and entirely forgetting they'd been born to so-called Polite Society. They also involved quite a lot of nudity.

In the end, he had to admit that perhaps they were less scenarios and more outright fantasies. For one thing, where would the servants who lived at Idlewood go? For another, he and Eliza were still strangers to each other.

All this time, he'd thought of nothing more than the stain his late uncle had left upon the family. Now it was time to look to the future. To the next generation.

How long would it take him to conceive a child with his wife?

If the erection he sported at the thought was any indication, he could only hope it wouldn't happen too quickly.

The best remedy for a long couple of days of riding was to be ridden. But he and his wife didn't know each other. Oh, he'd been ridden by strangers before, plenty of times. Women whose names he couldn't remember—names he might not have learned to begin with.

This was different. It was a lot to expect from a virgin raised to be a lady. He had to get to know her first. That seemed like a reasonable first step. But how?

It was up to him to make her satisfactorily confident in the marital bed. Would it be possible to bring her up to scratch? Or would she be shocked and pull away from him, believing that the act was a necessary evil to be endured?

Jeremy turned at the sound of a shout. One of his tenants, Mr. Boden, was chasing a small flock of runaway lambs—that were headed directly for a rocky slope. No dogs were in sight.

Without thinking, Jeremy was off his horse in an instant. He tied the reins to a post, tossed his hat aside, and shucked his damnably tight jacket, then hopped the partially constructed fence.

These were not the small, newborn lambs of January and February, those creatures little more than skin, bones, a panicked bleat, and an instinct to suckle with all their might. These were the lambs that had, these past three or four months, grown fat and strong—and fast—on their mothers' milk. They would not be easy to wrangle.

Catching each of the creatures alone without a net—and a rather large net, at that—would have been impossible. If there were two or three, he might have stood a chance. But there were nine or ten. They were going to fall and be injured, or worse, unless he could divert them. Even one was too valuable to lose. They each meant meat, wool, or breeding. The perfect ewe meant all three.

He charged at them, yelling and waving his hands. The small grouping divided. Several ran right past him, heedless of the threat he posed. Several more turned toward the enclosure where they could be herded into a safe space, as he'd hoped they would, while the last remaining made a mad dash for the road.

It was not going well.

Jeremy's blood pounded in his ears, his heart clawing the inside of his chest in desperation. At the back of his mind was the thought that this wasn't how he wanted his bride to see either him or Idlewood on the first day.

In fact, this fiasco was something of a personal nightmare. It represented everything he fought each and every day to avoid.

Loss of control.

Chapter Six

Eliza stood in the road outside the carriage with Christiana on one side and Margaret on the other as an unimaginable scene played out before them.

A man in his shirtsleeves. Not a sight she was accustomed to seeing. It was, however, a sight not soon forgotten.

Lord Bennington—an *earl*, of all people—was in the derelict field going after the runaway lambs. The billowing sleeves of his white linen undershirt emphasized the way the waistcoat hugged the lean taper of his torso. His quick and decisive movements displayed a strong and confident athleticism.

Whatever that was worth, for his abilities didn't seem to be helping him with the lambs. What had been one group divided into three.

Eliza tore her gaze from the earl and grasped her cousin's arm. She had to take charge. "We must do something."

Christiana's face set in resolute determination. She nodded. Then her expression shifted, her brows going up, her mouth softening out of its hard line of conviction. "But what?"

Margaret touched her arm. "My lady, it wouldn't be safe."

"What are *lambs* going to do to me, Margaret?" Confidence rang in the easy words. Or bravado, more like. She'd spent her life under a domineering and disagreeable mother. Compared to Lady Rushworth, what damage could lambs do? They couldn't crush a spirit.

True, animals were unpredictable and often much stronger than they looked, even when they weren't frightened out of their slender wits. But standing by and doing nothing—well, that would have been wrong.

The servant's eyes begged her to see reason. "Please let the men—"

There was a shout. Lord Bennington was signaling to the farmer.

Three of the lambs were charging for the road—directly toward them.

One of the chestnut horses whinnied and tried to shy away. The second horse responded to his companion's nervousness with a shake of his head.

She had to trust the coachman to keep them under control. The last thing they needed in this mayhem was the horses to bolt.

"Quickly, quickly." Eliza motioned to her cousin. The lambs were fast approaching. They had precious little time. "We'll cage them inside the carriage."

"The carriage? How in the world are we supposed to get them into the carriage?"

The coachman jumped down from his seat. He was small and hunched from a lifetime perched on the seat and sported bluish-gray pouches below each eye. "My lady, I wouldn't dream of interfering..." His dark expression betrayed the lie behind his words. It seemed very much as if he wanted to give Eliza a piece of his mind, whether or not she was the new countess.

But she *was* the countess. So she ignored him. "Margaret, you go to the other side and hold the door shut so they can't escape that way."

The maid rushed away without arguing.

The coachman stepped forward, more insistent this time. "My lady—"

"You see to the horses, my good man—go now."

His teeth set, but he followed the order. To do otherwise would have been an affront.

Eliza's attention whipped back to her cousin. "Christiana, you go to that side and be threatening so they don't go that way, and I'll go to that side so they don't go that way. They'll have no choice but to go into the carriage, and then we'll shut the door on them."

Her heart pounded. Every sense was on high alert.

It wasn't the stupidest thing she'd ever done. No, on a strictly linear scale that prize was reserved for having married the earl under false pretenses. But this wasn't far behind.

Before she knew what was happening, the lambs bounded one way. Christiana yelled. Then they bounded the other way. Eliza yelled.

And then they bounded right up into the carriage.

"Go! Go!" Eliza dashed for the door and reached it at the same time as Christiana.

They slammed the carriage shut. Christiana pinned herself against the door so they couldn't escape, and Eliza followed suit.

The trapped animals bleated and cried. In their panicked state, they threw themselves around the confined space with such ferocity that the entire conveyance shook back and forth on its springs.

A pair of hooved feet beat against the glass, cracking the delicate pane. Then shards flew everywhere.

"I don't know how long we can hold them." In her haste to help, Eliza hadn't considered that penning the lambs might exacerbate their excitement.

Her bonnet was askew, partially obscuring her vision. Christiana's had vanished entirely, and the seam of her sleeve had split around the elbow.

On the other side of the carriage, Margaret screamed. There was the sound of cracking wood, and suddenly the lambs were free again, racing down the road, kicking up a cloud of dust in their wake.

Watching them go, Eliza's shoulders sank.

Margaret came from around the other side, an unusual display of shock on her features. "Forgive me, my lady. I couldn't hold them."

The maid was such a small creature, Eliza should have gone around to help her instead of staying with Christiana.

"There is nothing to forgive. You did your best."

Eliza turned to the carriage and winced. In a matter of seconds, three frightened lambs had done considerable damage. The seats and curtains were in tatters, the wood beaten and broken, the glass shattered. Clumps of hard mud from their hooves littered the floor, and the door on Margaret's side hung from one hinge.

She leaned inside the door and sniffed. No hint of sheep smell, though. In light of the destruction, that was something small for which to be grateful.

Every thought vanished as Lord Bennington approached, a storm of epic proportions written on his features. His brows were low, his jewel-toned gaze dangerous as his dark stare mentally sliced her to pieces.

It seemed there would be consequences for her, too.

Eliza's insides trembled. It had been a very, very long time since even her mother's wrath had had an effect upon her—any at all, never mind one so profound.

Her mother, however, could never be pleased. The earl, by contrast, seemed as if he *could* be. There was no small pang of desperation in Eliza's innermost heart that she would someday make him proud of her. An absurd thought, considering her deception. The most she could dare hope for was that he didn't despise her for the whole remainder of their lives.

Not about to let him guess at what he might be inflicting upon her, intensity of his glower or no, she planted her feet firmly on the dirt. She'd stand the ground she had every right to defend. She'd tried to help. It hadn't gone as planned. Nothing more to say.

It was miserably unfair that he be in such a state of disarray and still look so impossibly beautiful. Suddenly awash in self-consciousness, she brushed at her skirts and set her bonnet to rights.

"We'll talk about this later." His voice was low and lethal. Lord Bennington took the reins of his horse and swung himself upon the mount, leaving Eliza in agony to guess what was to come.

Chapter Seven

In the house, Eliza allowed Margaret to set her to rights and called for a bath.

The servants proved eager to bring the buckets required. That boded well for a staff working under a master they respected. They filed in and out, clothing clean and pressed, hair and caps neat, posture excellent. Bright inquisitiveness sparkled from their eyes, but none of them addressed her, except to show their deference. If they were half so curious about Eliza as she was about them and her new life, they were managing themselves magnificently.

The polished tin tub was enormous. Bigger than anything Eliza had imagined could exist. Specially made for the earl himself, the housekeeper had explained.

Sinking into the steaming-hot water was akin to resigning her bone-weary self to the care of an angel's soft wing.

A thought stirred her as she soaked. She was naked in the same tub where the earl, too, had been naked. Was it wrong that she wanted to imagine him without clothing? Remembering the display of raw masculinity when he'd torn away his jacket and run to corral the lambs stirred her in places she had no business being stirred. They might be married, but they had a long road ahead when she revealed the truth about herself. Matters were muddled enough as it was. Then there was the business with the lambs and the carriage to muck it up all the more.

Eliza was by the fire running a comb through her damp hair to dry it when Christiana slipped in. Her cousin, well groomed and properly attired in a rosy afternoon dress, gaped. She blinked through her spectacles. "What a room!"

The words brought a stinging heat to Eliza's cheeks. Indeed, she had been well used to fine things in life. She was the daughter of an earl herself, after all, but she was not the least bit ignorant of the privilege of her birth and position. Although it seemed she lived in a world where everyone had the best of everything, that was an illusion. The accident of birth had made her one of the select few to be sheltered in finery and endless comforts.

The accident of marriage was bringing her deeper into that world. The mistress's bedchamber at Idlewood had not been made with a countess in mind. It had been made for a princess.

The room was done in a dusky blue, and the centerpiece was the large bed, carved with intricate designs and scrollwork and hung with rich velvets and gold cord. The walls were silk, the ornamentation gilded, the rugs unthinkably plush, and the fireplace where she now sat an exquisite copper-yellow marble that outright glowed in the firelight.

This line of the Landon family might have been ruined once, but it appeared to have recovered rather well. Which, considering the earl's afternoon display, made all the sense in the world. Any man who did what he'd done was full of rigid determination and not afraid to go to any lengths.

Eliza couldn't think of any response to the exclamation,

so she changed the subject. "How are you, cousin?"

"My nerves are a jumble." Christiana took a chair and placed it opposite Eliza, letting out a sigh before speaking. By the fire, her flame-colored hair assumed a new dimension. "I keep doubting myself. I was heartbroken when I thought I'd have to marry Lord Bennington. But then you did, and I'm consumed by fear and guilt. I'm beginning to think it will be impossible for me to be happy because of what you did, which increases my guilt tremendously. And I keep thinking about what is going to happen when he discovers the truth. Or worse—when my aunt realizes what you've done."

"My mother can't change anything any more than we can." It was the same bitter lesson she'd learned upon giving away her virginity. Foolish child she'd been, thinking herself to be in love with an oily scoundrel. His careful seduction started, she realized in retrospect, when he'd discovered she'd liked cherries. He'd used it as an excuse to pick them and bring her pretty little baskets filled with the fruit.

To this day, the taste and feel of cherries in her mouth made her gag.

"I'm sorry I called him a horrid old earl, cousin. He's not quite so horrid as all that. Or so old."

"I'd already forgotten."

"I can't imagine a worse beginning to your first day at Idlewood." Christiana twirled an artfully stray curl at the nape of her neck.

"Surely the limits of your imagination extend beyond madly frightened lambs and a ruined carriage." The statement was a deflection—an attempt at being lighthearted without overlooking the fact that the day was undoubtedly going to get worse. Much worse. Lord Bennington still had no idea whom he'd married.

"Oh, frightened lambs and ruined carriages are well outside the bounds of my imagination, I assure you." Christiana smiled—the first impish smile on her face since before she'd become the ward of Lady Rushworth. With the tip of one finger, she pushed her spectacles back up her nose. "What are you going to wear for your first dinner at Idlewood?"

Eliza hadn't been thinking about her gown. Her mind was on the jewels, the ones hidden in her trunks. "Oh, I'll find something, I'm sure."

"Shall I help you?"

"Tomorrow, perhaps. Tonight any old thing will do."

Christiana looked taken aback. "But it's your first night at Idlewood as the new countess."

"And everybody will be tired after traveling and all the more weary after what happened with the lambs."

After Christiana left her bedchamber, Eliza, heavy with renewed guilt, pushed aside the shifts and stockings packed in the trunk and withdrew a wide, flat box from behind the false bottom. With reverent care, she placed it on the surface of the dressing table. Taking a tiny key hidden in the secret drawer of the box of toilette items, she unlatched the lock.

The necklace, bracelet, and earrings her father had given her were hidden within. The diamonds were the color of fine champagne, their facets throwing off the light as she gently picked up the necklace and placed it about her throat.

She'd been fourteen the day her father had presented her with the box. He'd been shining with pride. "I'd given these to old Bennington for safekeeping. Today I got them back."

"Why did you give something to Lord Bennington for safekeeping?" she'd asked. Given her mother's open animosity for the Landon family, the earl had seemed a strange choice. It was a question she'd puzzled over for a time and then forgotten about until she stood with the new Lord Bennington as his bride.

"Never mind that, Eliza."

At the time, she'd assumed it'd had something to do with

her mother. Something she didn't care to think about...well, at all, really.

Then he'd opened the box. She'd gasped at the sparkling array.

"You'll look beautiful in these, my girl," he'd said. And then he'd paused, considering her, his eyes misting and his voice cracking as he added, "You always look beautiful, adorned or not, because your true beauty resides in the depths of your heart."

The day she'd received them, she'd imagined being old enough to wear them. Later she'd despaired of ever doing so—knowing her mistake had cost her the life she'd been meant to lead. How her father's words had haunted her. Her true beauty...something she'd sullied irrevocably the day she'd allowed that wretched man to ruin her, naught but a few months after her father had given her the jewels. And with her virginity went her chance to ever be truly loved. For a while, she'd hoped things might be different. That there might be hope for her yet. Foolish. Captain Pearson had taught her only too well how wrong she'd been.

A thousand times she'd dreamed of selling the stones and starting her own life away from her mother. Twice, she'd even smuggled them to a jeweler's, only to find herself outside the door, feet stuck to the ground, unable to walk inside. Her father had always appeared in her mind, his pained expression all too clear.

As she placed the stones around her throat, Eliza drew in a breath and tried to wipe her mind of all these maudlin thoughts. She was *not* going to feel sorry for herself, she was not.

For all their troubles, Eliza knew that her father would have wanted her to care for her mother. To be a good daughter, no matter how terribly she'd fouled herself in the past. Which only increased the burden of guilt for her latest transgression.

Marrying Lord Bennington was as good as abandoning her mother, just as selling the jewels and running away would have been.

"I miss you, Father," she whispered, studying her reflection as she lightly fingered the stones.

She frowned. They didn't look right. Maybe it was because the diamonds represented one more deception—a secret she'd kept from her mother at her father's request. He hadn't wanted Lady Rushworth to know they weren't to be hers, deciding instead to save them for his daughter. Eliza had given her word, but she'd struggled with the guilt of the secret for years. Her mother would be crushed if she ever discovered the duplicity.

Lord Bennington wouldn't know. It was their first night together at Idlewood. It should have been the right occasion.

But it wasn't.

Slowly, with some regret, Eliza returned the necklace to the box, turned the lock, and tucked them behind the dressing table.

They would need to be better hidden, but she could think about that after dinner. Or—she stifled a yawn—perhaps tomorrow morning.

Tonight, there was an entire evening to endure. She would have to look her husband in the eye and admit she'd lied. She'd have to see the hurt and anger on his face. Whatever the consequences to her actions, she'd have to face them.

Chapter Eight

In his bedchamber after an all but interminable evening, Jeremy let his valet help him out of his jacket. If what had passed tonight was a look into his marital future, he was going to have to make a few adjustments.

He reminded himself again and again that he barely knew his wife. Yet church and Society sanctioned them to share one another's beds and bodies.

That left the question of whether or not he had one all-important thing—the most important blessing of all. His wife's. Would she welcome him into her bed? Or would she merely endure his…what would they be between them? Husbandly attentions?

His stomach curdled at the unfortunate terminology. Once begun, he'd never before experienced trouble completing the deed. But even he might have trouble staying hard in the face of *that* unfortunate nomenclature and all it entailed.

He wanted a good, fast rut. The kind that left them both flushed, and breathless, and trembling from pleasure.

"It's all right, Yates." Jeremy went to work on the cuffs of his sleeves, a curling lock of hair falling over his brow when he bent his head. "I can manage the rest myself."

"As you wish, my lord."

The slim figure of the servant slipped from the room.

Leaving Jeremy to the unfortunate company of the decision before him.

Dressed in nothing but his banyan, he stared at the door joining his bedchamber to his wife's. Should he wander through? He was master of the place, after all.

No, surely not. He was the master of Idlewood and the earl, but he wasn't an oaf. He had to knock. Eliza had a choice in this matter, after all.

He raised his hand. But didn't rap his knuckles against the door.

What did other newly married couples do? He and she weren't the first to have married without knowing aught of each other.

Pulling back, he ran his fingers through his hair. Why was this so difficult?

He looked down. Maybe it would be easier if he weren't sporting such a bloody obvious proof of his arousal. Usually, a wooden cock was just the thing. But with a *wife* who'd been raised as a lady?

It was unlikely she was used to thinking of people as having carnal natures and core animal compulsions. His carnal nature and core animal compulsions were almost too much for him—his greatest shortcoming and the genesis of all his greatest sins. They could easily land him on the wrong side of heaven.

He was going to have to hide that part of himself from his wife. She could never find out how profound his needs were. It was going to be difficult, but he'd cultivated control his entire life. Now it mattered more than ever.

Hell. A wedding night wasn't supposed to be so difficult.

The equation wasn't complicated. A man was supposed to slip into his wife's bed, and then into her body.

There was but a single thing to do.

He knocked.

• • •

Eliza started at the sound of the knock. This was it. He was coming, and they hadn't even had time to discuss…well, *anything*.

She made a dash for the bed, blowing out the beeswax candle with a quick puff of air and hauling the heavy coverings up to her chin. Her book hadn't made it to the bedside table, but there were many instances of having slept the entire night with a tome lost in the blankets. Nothing to trouble herself over.

In the dark silence, she cursed. Why hadn't she simply opened the door? It wasn't as if she could escape the inevitable revelation of truths under the pack of lies.

Oh, but she had so many sins for which to atone. All of them against her husband—and they hadn't yet been married a full three days.

There was another knock.

Eliza scrambled to sit up fully while yanking the counterpane to keep herself properly covered. The book fell away, sliding down the bed. It landed on the floor with a jarring *thump*, abusing her chafed nerves. "You may enter."

Oh, no. She'd done it. She'd told him to come in—into her bedchamber. Where he was going to expect…

Lord Bennington appeared holding a candle. "Do I disturb you, my lady?" There seemed to be tension in his voice.

"What are you doing here?"

Immediately, she winced. Of all the ludicrous things she

could have said. He was going to think her a simpleton. Or worse—too sheltered to know what happened between a man and a woman. One heard of that happening from time to time. Some poor girl raised under absurd notions of purity and innocence. It seemed horribly cruel, to both her and the man she married.

Eliza wanted to sink back into the bed and disappear.

The earl stood frozen, shock on his strong features. "I—er—thought we should…should talk about the lambs."

Eliza blinked. Then she bit her bottom lip. Hard. If she hadn't, she'd have burst out laughing. Poor man was probably in agony for having blurted that so thoughtlessly. "The lambs, you say?"

"You…orchestrated a rather…"

No doubt he hated himself about now. She would, were their situations reversed.

"I was trying to help. I'm sorry it turned out the way it did, but I wasn't about to sit by and watch." His discomfiture made her bold. She was going to test his limits. She nodded to the door behind him to see how he'd react to being dismissed. Either he'd leave or it would push him toward the truth of why he'd come. "If that's all, my lord, it's been a long and wearying day."

He stepped a few paces into the room and stopped, running his fingers through his hair.

"Actually, that's not all. I realize we never talked about this…" He cleared his throat. "And this is a terrible time to do so, I realize, and I am sorry, but I was wondering if…if you might like it if we…" He raised his brows significantly, gesturing as if trying to find the words in the air. "Well, if you might like to…"

If she might like *to…?*

That was not the question Eliza had been expecting. She'd been thinking all day about whether or not he would ask to come to her bed. If, indeed, he did ask—he didn't have to do so. He was her husband. He had his rights. But something told her Lord Bennington wasn't the sort of man to inflict harm on anyone, not for any reason.

She hadn't considered for a moment whether or not she would *like* to. She swallowed. "I'm fully prepared to give you an heir, my lord."

"That wasn't my question."

Why did he have to press the point? He couldn't expect her to admit her feelings on the matter, could he? She hardly knew them herself.

Except she did, didn't she? Even if she didn't want to admit them to herself, they were there. There was something about the earl that was different from any other man she'd ever known. Something that stirred her in places she hadn't thought could be roused after what she'd done all those years ago. "That's the best I can do, I'm afraid. We...we might as well, I suppose."

"We might as well?"

"We have a duty to see to, and there's but one way about it."

"A duty." His voice had gone flat.

Without warning, he proffered a stiff bow and left, closing the door behind him.

Eliza fell back against her pillows and stared into the blackness. Putting off the conversation one more day would make it ever so much more awkward. She squeezed her eyes shut and heaved a sigh. The longer they went with her deception intact, the worse everything was going to be.

Chapter Nine

Well before breakfast the following morning, Templeton stood in the doorway of the alcove adjacent the library where Jeremy was trying to work. "Has the present for her ladyship arrived?"

"Indeed it has, my lord."

Jeremy threw the land manager's report on the neatly arranged desk before him. Thank heaven for the interruption. Being tied to the Bennington title meant he kept an extremely close eye on all business and estate matters. But with his wife weighing heavily on his mind, he hadn't accomplished one single, solitary thing.

It didn't happen often that he couldn't concentrate on matters at hand, but when it did, it was nothing but irritating.

One thing plagued his thoughts: what to do about getting into his wife's bed. Did they need to talk? Was she simply going to be expecting him tonight? Did she still expect their union to be *chaste*? Devil take him, but he'd rather have his nails ripped out of their beds one by one than have that be the case. Although, when he'd first come into her room, she *had* said she'd been prepared to give him an heir, so perhaps marital chastity wasn't something he had to worry about.

Desperate for a reprieve from the maelstrom in his mind, Jeremy followed the sounds of women's delighted squeals and found himself in a part of Idlewood into which he rarely ventured. He stopped at the door outside a small drawing room.

The scene before him elicited an unexpected warmth in the center of his chest. His wife and her maid were exclaiming over the present. The King Charles Spaniel pup yipped and wagged its tail as its new mistress threw a toy that appeared to have been hastily made of old ribbons.

Eliza laughed. Her cheeks were rosy, her eyes sparkling. His gaze caught on her—and held. That first morning he'd seen her, she'd taken his breath away. But that was nothing to how beautiful she was now.

From his stance on the perimeter, Jeremy smiled.

"I see you like your gift, my lady."

The maid sobered and dropped her gaze as she dipped a curtsy. The puppy yipped and danced at Eliza's feet, trying to regain his mistress's attention and resume playing. She scooped the creature into her arms to scratch its ears and place a kiss on its head. "I couldn't be more delighted with her, my lord. Thank you."

"Oh, but—"

"How did you know that I always wanted a dog?"

"Ah. There, I must confess to subterfuge. I inquired with your maid." He left out the part about having a conversation with the servant about her role in taking notes back and forth between them before they married. As it turned out, the woman was remarkably loyal. He couldn't fault her for that.

"I should have guessed as much." Eliza beamed at the puppy and then at Margaret. The maid returned the smile with one of her own—wide with unfettered pleasure.

He was almost sidetracked by the abrupt understanding that his wife was going to make an excellent mother.

The warmth in Eliza's eyes as she cast him a shy look could have tempted him to hell. "I've decided to call her Daisy."

Jeremy cleared his throat and spoke reluctantly, not wanting to mar the moment. "Except it's a male dog, my lady."

Both the women's smiles vanished as they reexamined the little dog, who clearly enjoyed the attention. He wiggled and squirmed upward in Eliza's arms, trying to lick her face.

Eliza gave a quick glance in the appropriate region. "Oh, I see, so he is." She concentrated on the dog's face. "I shall have to think of another name, it seems. What do you think, Margaret? Nothing immediately springs to mind."

"I'm sure I couldn't say, my lady." The barest hint of a rougher accent lingered in the servant's words. "I thought he made for a rather nice Daisy, if I do say so myself."

"Yes, so did I. Oh, well, 'tis no matter. I'm sure I shall think of something else for her. Him, I mean." She gave Jeremy a look, head slightly tilting to one side. "Was there something you came to see me about, my lord?"

Little more than whether or not she would agree to allow him into her bed. How did a man ask such a thing—and of his wife, no less? In all his previous interactions, the outcome had been obvious far enough in advance with naught more than a glance.

As if sensing she was no longer wanted, Margaret absented herself, head bowed in staid deference. Eliza threw the toy for the dog, who tripped over its legs in pursuit.

This was his chance. They were alone again. At dinner, too many servants would be about. Although he *could* dismiss them.

No. He struck the notion from his mind. It would be far too strange and uncomfortable to broach such a subject over a meal, even if they'd been truly alone. When servants were dismissed, they always vanished, but they never went far.

Tonight—all he needed to ask was if he could come to her tonight. They didn't need to go into the particulars. He was being straightforward enough to be understood without saying something that might embarrass them both.

The words didn't come.

He cleared his throat. She looked up from the puppy and raised her brows at him.

Lord help him, but he hadn't been tongue-tied like this in…well, he'd never been tongue-tied like this before, come to think of it. What needed to be discussed, he discussed, reasonably and sensibly.

Except how could he make demands of her? He wanted children. There was but one way to beget the next generation.

Smiling, Eliza kissed the squirming pup again, her attention lost to the little creature in her arms. While he had dithered, his moment to speak had slipped away.

"It's of no importance." Of no importance, his ass. His inner self seethed at his cowardice.

In an effort to redeem himself, he took a step forward. The last time they'd been so close, he'd kissed her. He had a mind to do it again.

She must have sensed his intention, for her cheeks darkened. The pink of her blush set off her hair, which only made him think of seeing the locks freed about her shoulders. "My lady, if you don't mind, I should very much like to…"

Not meeting his gaze, Eliza nodded and licked her lips, as if in anticipation. "Of course, my lord."

The awkwardness didn't diminish the need that had sprung up in him. Quite literally, in fact. What he wouldn't have given to shut the door, turn her around, and take her hard and fast over the back of his chair.

One did not do such things to virgins, however.

Their lips met. She was warm and smelled like Eden itself.

It would have been far too easy to have gotten carried away. He broke away. Tonight…tonight he would do better. He bowed with more gallantry than he felt like displaying in the face of enough potent need to drive him half mad. "I'll bid you a good rest of your day, my lady."

• • •

"A visitor, my lord."

At his desk, Jeremy set the letter down and attended Templeton. The butler's expression gave no hint as to what Jeremy should expect. "Not my brother, I hope."

Arthur had threatened to visit the couple after they were wed, which he undoubtedly would—when he wanted money.

"This young man says he has business with you concerning Miss Burke."

Miss Burke?

Jeremy squinted. "Am I supposed to know this woman in question?"

Templeton gave him a rare look.

"Oh. Right." Eliza before she had become his countess. So who was this young man? Surely not the man whom she'd professed to love.

A shadow fell over Jeremy's mood, and a swirl of conflicting emotions made him scowl. Jealousy and possessiveness mingled with regret for his callous disregard of his now wife's heart.

"Very well. I shall see him."

Jeremy stood and tugged the bottom hem of his waistcoat and brushed at the sleeves of his wool jacket to remove any stray specks.

A young man with a rectangular head and an all too shiny expression came into the library. His cheeks were pink with pleasure, and he wore a red coat.

No. It couldn't be. If Jeremy had married the woman this man loved, he would not appear so happy now. And he did look happy. Terribly so.

"You're Lord Bennington, I assume?"

"Indeed."

"I beg you to allow me the indulgence of shaking your hand, my lord."

Before he could answer, the man had crossed the room and taken Jeremy's hand within both of his own. "I can't thank you enough for what you did, my lord."

"For what I did?"

"For marrying her."

Befuddled, Jeremy stared. "Forgive me, but you have me at a disadvantage, I'm afraid."

"No, no. It's I who should be asking your forgiveness. My name is Lieutenant Hart. Tom Hart. And I am entirely indebted to you, my lord. I can't ever repay you."

"Come to the point, Lieutenant."

"For not marrying Christiana, of course."

Jeremy froze. *Not marrying Christiana?* A rock lodged itself in the center of his stomach. A man couldn't believe he was marrying one woman and instead marry an entirely different one. It wasn't done. The scandal…

He couldn't have heard correctly. "I'm sorry?"

Was it Jeremy's imagination, or did the man's grin actually *widen*?

"For not marrying Christiana. Miss Burke and I are to be married tomorrow. She'll be of age, and…well, being together, it's all we've dreamed of since…" The young lieutenant's cheer faltered, his smile wavering. Some of the color faded from his cheeks. "Are you…" He cleared his throat, brows sinking. "Are you quite well, my lord?"

The last thing Jeremy needed was this young man—this

stranger—seeing into his confusion. He couldn't lash out. He wouldn't. First, as of yet there was no evidence of his having colluded in any deception. Second, if there was one thing Jeremy relied upon, it was his capacity for control. A single slip was one too many.

"Forgive me, Lieutenant, but how did you get here so quickly?"

"Miss Burke and I have planned for several years to marry. We only had to wait for her to come of age. I was well on my way to London when she left. All I had to do was come a little farther—and no distance is too great where she is concerned."

"I see." Jeremy paused. The young man earnestly believed himself in love, didn't he? Well, far be it for Jeremy to challenge a man on his feelings, however absurd they might be. "Why don't you avail yourself of some refreshments? Are you staying in the village?"

Lieutenant Hart nodded. "At the Silver Lion, my lord."

"I'll send a messenger to pay your bill and have a room made up for you here."

The young man turned serious. "Oh, I don't think I could share a roof with Christiana before we're wed. Miss Burke, I mean. 'Twouldn't be proper. Thank you all the same, my lord."

"In a house like Idlewood, Lieutenant, it will all be perfectly honorable, I promise you. You're to be wed. You must allow me to share my hospitality. It's the least I can do in wishing you joy."

He stalked from the room to inform Templeton of the plans.

Afterward, in the silence of the corridor, he pressed a fist against the wall, letting the sturdy structure support part of his weight as he took slow breaths deep into his lungs.

This could not be happening.

It had to be something else. There had to be a

misunderstanding. He had to have misheard. Misconstrued. Something. Anything but what it had sounded like.

His teeth clenched. He had to talk to his wife. But not until the first flush of anger had subsided. As much as he wanted to charge in to see her immediately, he well knew what a foolish decision it would be. He had to let his blood cool before he saw her. Because the one thing that mattered most was that he remain master over himself.

Chapter Ten

Eliza was in the breakfast room when Christiana joined her.

Christiana beamed.

"A dog! You have a dog!" She knelt on the floor and tussled with the little creature, who yipped with joy. "What's her name?"

"Daisy."

"Oh, how perfect!" Daisy bounced down and trotted over to Christiana. "Look at those lovely brown eyes."

"Well…" Eliza went thoughtful a moment. It was difficult to look at the pup without sensing that under different circumstances she would have been grateful to marry the earl. She wasn't sorry, not exactly. But she didn't have the right to be happy. "Apparently, he's male and I have to think of another name, but—"

"What a shame."

"—I haven't been able to think of anything."

A few minutes later, over a plate piled with steaming food, her cousin opened a letter from a friend who was remaining in London until the end of the Season. While Eliza pushed food around her plate, Daisy remained by her feet, tongue lolling, eyes bright, in ever-vigilant hope of a crumb.

After last night, Eliza's conscience weighed far too heavily to eat. She had a confession to make.

The breakfast room at Idlewood mocked her with its simple beauty and elegance. The azure walls, the perfect draperies in a complementary cream shade that could have been straight from *Ackermann's Repository*, and the airy lines of the furniture. She was mistress of this place. But she had no right to be.

What would become of her when she told Lord Bennington of her deception?

There were the jewels, of course. After keeping them all these years, it would be terrible to be forced to part with them. If, however, the choice was between destitution and a modest existence in some quiet, out-of-the-way place, she'd have to do exactly that. If her father were still alive, he would understand.

Abandoning the food, Eliza took Daisy into her arms and went to the windows. The morning mists were burning away, revealing the promise of a sun-soaked May day. How horrible.

From behind her came a choking sound. Eliza turned to her cousin, eyes wide. "What is it? Are you all right?"

Christiana's cheeks had turned an alarming shade of red. She looked up from the letter over her spectacles, panic in her features. "It's going around London. Someone found out, and it's going around London."

Eliza needed no explanation. Her insides filled with cold lead. If Lord Bennington heard what she'd done from anyone but her…

"Already?"

She kicked herself. She should have told him straightaway. He had a right to know—a right to hear it from her, not from anyone else—and every second she waited, the risk grew higher.

Her head went light. Hadn't Templeton made mention of a visitor coming to see the earl earlier this morning?

Steady. The earl was a busy man. It could have been any number of people. She wouldn't let her imagination gallop wildly ahead of any solid evidence.

Daisy in her arms, Eliza left the breakfast room in a resolute stride. But Lord Bennington wasn't where she expected him. The library was empty.

Back in the corridor, she found the butler down at the other end, deep in discussion with the head footman.

"Mr. Templeton, if you please." Both men stopped what they were doing to acknowledge her. "Where might I find his lordship?"

"I believe he's gone for a turn in the gardens, my lady. Incidentally, his lordship asked me to tell you that he requires you to join him there as soon as you're finished."

Her stomach dropped. Why had she been such a foolish coward? She shouldn't have waited. She should have told him everything without delay.

Eliza was still tying the ribbons to secure her bonnet when she slipped from the house onto the gray flagstones of a large terrace. Daisy followed at her heels.

Lord Bennington wasn't visible. But the gardens were extensive. He could be anywhere.

She set out. Daisy immediately darted out down the path with a happy yip, ears flying. The dog stopped partway down to look back at Eliza. Then, apparently content, she turned her attention to a small pond rimmed in stone. She lapped the water, the silky plume of her tail wagging the entire time.

Despite everything, Eliza couldn't help but smile. She'd had Daisy no more than a few hours, but the sweet creature was everything she'd wanted in an animal companion.

The earl must have gone to some trouble to transport the

dog to Idlewood so quickly. Whatever was to come after her confession, she wasn't going to be parted from Daisy. If the earl threw her out without the slightest compunction, the dog would come with her.

Eliza took a few steps then turned down a path lined with cherry laurel, the glossy leaves casting off the bright morning sunlight.

Perhaps tossing her out was the very worst case—the scenario for which she was trying to prepare herself to make the real consequences of her actions, whatever they would be, less dreadful.

The Landons being as averse to scandal as they were, it seemed unlikely that he'd do something so drastic.

Then again, she didn't know the man. They'd shared two kisses—well, one and a half, more like—which didn't mean much, no matter what they'd stirred in her.

And just like that, around the corner, she stopped short.

He was hunched close to the ground, attending something one of the gardeners was explaining. The bed before them had recently been dug up, piles of earth overturned to reveal a rich, deep brown. Wheelbarrows, uprooted plants, and various tools were strewn about the area.

The earl rose at the sight of her. The gardener straightened. He didn't wait to be dismissed but excused himself with a bow.

Set against the blue sky with Idlewood behind him, Lord Bennington's height seemed exaggerated. It had to be a trick of the mind—a manifestation of her fear. He was large, certainly, but not a giant.

Daisy ran to stand before Eliza's feet and yipped as if protecting her—his, rather—mistress from a threat.

Which he might have been, for all Eliza knew.

When the earl spoke, his voice was low. "We need to talk, my lady. A young Lieutenant Hart arrived this morning and said something quite interesting."

Her mouth went dry. The sun was suddenly too bright. The birds too horribly cheerful. The earl far too much of a stranger—a stranger she'd misled in a dreadful fashion.

But that wasn't the worst of it, was it? If he was this angry now at discovering her deception, what would he do when she confessed her lack of virginity?

Captain Pearson's words clawed at the inside of her skull. *Why would any man want a whore like you?* He had looked at her with such disgust.

She'd brought this upon herself. The very moment she'd put her name on the paper in answer to the earl's demand that she tell him her name, she'd known there would be a reckoning.

And here it was.

• • •

Jeremy watched with cool interest. His wife's expression was troubled, her color a bit too pale for the bright and beautiful day, and her composure distinctly disturbed.

Yet she still stood before him. That took some doing.

Whenever he witnessed a person doing what she didn't want to do but was determined to do anyway, he couldn't help but admire her.

"Whatever it is you have to say"—he spoke with quiet care—"I want to hear it."

She looked down. "There's something you ought to know."

Jeremy's abdominals clenched. Here it was. The admission. Was he ready to hear it?

The Landons had scandal in spades, and the previous earl wasn't alone. He had company. *Plenty* of company. First, the old earl's daughter Grace had had an accidental encounter in a storeroom with a man. That had set tongues dancing merrily, even though that man was now her husband. Then there was Phoebe. She'd married a rambunctious scoundrel whose sordid family history rivaled even the Landons'.

Unfortunately, it didn't end there. Oh, no. There was *also* the business of yet another Landon sister, Isabel. Whom Jeremy couldn't think about without becoming angry with his mother for having abetted her wild scheme. The consolation was that Isabel's secret life remained unknown. So far. It was a house of cards waiting to be destroyed by the lightest breeze.

He braced himself. He'd worked too hard for too long to allow another scandal to harm the family. Unwittingly, he'd found himself in the middle of one. Marriage by deceit. That he could never forgive.

"I'm not Lady Rushworth's ward."

"No?" He didn't feign surprise.

"No."

Jeremy scowled, finally able to voice the question plaguing him since his conversation with young Hart. "Then who are you?"

It was a devil of a thing to have to ask one's own wife. But he sincerely didn't know.

"I'm her daughter."

Chapter Eleven

The air vanished from Jeremy's lungs. It was as if he'd been punched in the gut.

Her daughter? Eliza was Lady Rushworth's *daughter*?

Dear sweet holy heaven. He'd married the daughter of the person who hated him most in all the world.

A swift flood of boiling anger threatened to drown him. Part of him wanted to laugh. Another part wanted to slam his fist into stone and shatter rock to dissipate the violent assault of rage. His teeth clenched, and he was trembling as he fought for air. "You deceived me. In the worst possible way."

She paled and bent her head. "I know."

"Are you not sorry for what you've done?"

She raised her head, eyes shining with defiance. "I couldn't let you marry Christiana. She loves Tom."

Jeremy had not expected this. In light of this startling revelation, he must maintain control. He'd spent far too long gaining mastery over the hotheaded youth who'd used a wooden sword on an innocent tree to vent his anger and frustration. He wasn't under anyone else's domination. He was the master now. And when the time came, he'd be nothing like his own father had been to him.

It was by far the biggest test he'd endured in some time. Perhaps even his biggest test to date. "It's about her? You did this to *me* for *her*?"

"Yes."

It was too simple. He wanted...well, he didn't know what he wanted. But it wasn't this. "That's it, then? You cared so much for your cousin's future that you sacrificed your own?"

"I have no future, my lord."

Something about the way she spoke the lines—plainly, but with a measure of resignation—the sadness of her words pricked against the cold husk of his heart. He waved as if to at once dismiss the sensation and the notion. "That's absurd. You're the daughter of an earl, are you not? And an heiress."

She only pressed her lips together. "I wasn't doing terribly on my own. Spinsterhood agreed with me, I dare say."

His instinct to smash something warred with the last vestiges of rational thought that screamed at him to maintain control—especially in front of her. Somehow he'd stepped close enough to be looming over her. Close enough, too, to catch the scent of roses on her.

A breeze swept through, rustling the detritus strewn about the ground. In the wind, the fabric of her skirts clung about her legs, revealing their length and shape. Jeremy's stance must have upset the dog he'd given her, for the creature abandoned the stray leaves he'd been chasing and came to stand at Eliza's feet, staring at Jeremy as if protecting his mistress.

"We're not going to talk about this here in the middle of the gardens." Jeremy tempered his tone, taking a deep lungful of air in an attempt to burst free of the vines of rage squeezing the breath out of him. "Let's go to the orangery."

He indicated the way and, after she scooped the dog into her arms, she followed the path toward the building. She slowed as they neared. "Is that really where we're going?"

The orangery was in a severe state of neglect. The glass was dirty and broken. Vines had overgrown the far end, and everything else had been left to die and rot where it stood.

"It's something I haven't gotten to yet." It was one of the final things remaining. "But it's safe enough inside, I promise you."

She stepped in carefully, keeping the dog close to her body, even when the little creature wiggled to free himself, too curious for his own good.

"It's strange that the house is so lovely and this has been completely ignored."

"It's unnecessary." If he sounded short, it was because he was in no mood to discuss his choices for rebuilding the estate.

She turned to look back over her shoulder, expression unreadable. "That seems a strange thing to decide."

He followed her inside. "I want to know who else knows about this."

"About our marriage?"

"About the fact that you deceived me into marrying you when I was meant to marry Christiana."

"You paid a debt by marriage. I daresay you got off pretty well, all things considered. And because I have it on very good authority that you don't have a heart, what difference does it make *whom* you married?"

"Did your mother have you do this to revenge herself upon me?"

"You didn't answer my question."

"I'm the one allowed to demand answers here, my lady. Not you."

Eliza looked him dead in the eye. "My mother knows *nothing* about it. Or didn't, before we left London."

"How am I supposed to believe you after what you've done?"

She threw her arms up in exasperation. "First you demand answers and then you throw doubt upon my responses? How am I supposed to reason with you if that's your tactic?"

"I can hardly believe this. I could never have conceived of such a thing, and here for the past few days…" He could only shake his head. At least this explained how pale she'd been after they'd married. "How could you do it?"

She licked her lips and softened her reply. "I admit, I didn't do a very good thing."

He almost choked on crazed laughter. "That's putting it mildly."

"You think I wanted this? I wrote you those letters. I begged you to call it off. They didn't work, but I dearly wish with every last fiber of my being that they had. You had no mercy for my position." Eliza glared.

She dearly wished the letters had worked, did she? *She* had tricked *him* into marriage and *she* was the one with regrets? "You think to gain my sympathy?"

"I think nothing of the sort. But you should be made fully aware of what this looks like from my perspective. It was wrong, tricking you into marrying me, but I did it for the right reason."

"First, there is nothing you or anyone can say to convince me of that. Second, there is nothing in the world to convince me your logic is the least bit justified."

"Would you really rather have married her? She loves someone else."

"So I've been told. And the nuptials will be tomorrow, apparently. He's here now. I met him."

"Then you must see that she needs him. She needs someone soft. Someone caring. Not a beast like you. You'd have cowed her when you flew into a temper like you just did."

"I do *not* fly into tempers." If she didn't heed the lethal note in his voice, there would be hell to pay. If he did, he'd renege on all the promises he'd made to himself to remain in control at all times. More importantly, what he promised himself he would not become—a man like his father, who'd nearly crushed his mother's soul before he'd had the good grace to die.

"I hate to be the one to disillusion you, my lord, but you're in a temper now." Eliza sounded anything but sorry.

He turned, momentarily unable to face her because he was afraid of saying "sod it" to the whole business and just kissing her.

Among the broken pots and overturned plants of the long-neglected orangery was a rosebush that had survived neglect. It'd grown tall and wild, taking over part of the framing on a partially collapsed wall. The pink buds were just beginning to open.

It was horribly symbolic. Like the angry and vengeful God of the Old Testament was sending Jeremy a pointed message.

Thankfully, Jeremy didn't believe in such things. It was no more than happenstance. What he *chose* to read into what he saw was entirely on him.

He turned back to Eliza, broken glass crunching under the soles of his boots. "So you're the better choice, then, are you?"

Daisy—which isn't how Jeremy wanted to think of the dog, but it would have to do until a better name came along—squirmed out of Eliza's arms and went to bark at a stray ginger cat that was sunning itself within the perfectly sized confines of an overturned table. The cat looked at Daisy with its ears back and gave the dog one good swat on the nose. Daisy yelped in shock and retreated.

"In the circumstance, my lord, there was no choice. I would have done far worse and far more than *marry you*"—she nearly spat the words—"to prevent so wretched and wrong a thing as a union between the pigheaded Lord Bennington and the sweet-tempered and lovely woman who is my s—cousin, Christiana."

"First beast. Now pigheaded." Part of what she said prickled at his conscience in a way he didn't care to examine. This woman he'd taken to wife had *deceived* him. There was no justification for it. None in the world. So there was no point in considering the fact that the idea of being eternally wed to Christiana made his cock want to run and hide in the corner whimpering instead of stretching long and hard like it did around Eliza. That wasn't the important part of marriage—what happened in the bedroom or how much one did or did not desire one's wife. He narrowed his eyes. "What a fine opinion you have of me. Under the circumstances, you might want to rethink your approach, my lady."

She raised her brows at him and smiled. In the glow of the morning light, he could have mistaken her for a wicked angel sent by heaven to torment him with her shimmering strength and perfect beauty. "I've spent too much of my life holding my tongue. I don't think it's done a spot of good. From here on out, I plan to speak my mind. I won't be silenced for *your* comfort, my lord."

"You give your mother respect that you don't give your husband?"

Her eyes went huge, and she snorted. "Respect? The last thing you've done here today, my lord, is earn my respect."

He opened his mouth to reply, but she rushed to continue.

"I will say this, my lord. I respect you enough that I promise you that I will never—never—give you deference in situations when it would behoove you to be taken to task, instead. And if you don't see that for the honor it is, you're not a man I could ever give my respect."

Her words took some of the heat out of his anger. *Some.* Certainly not all. This was too big. Her words were well aimed, but her deception was too much. What sort of woman dared do such a thing?

The question was poorly timed, because she licked her lips. It was just the tip of her pink tongue wetting that pretty bottom lip. A part of his brain he didn't want to acknowledge rushed to answer him. The sort of woman who dared do such a thing was a woman he wanted to kiss. Again.

He really was going mad, wasn't he?

She raised her chin at him. "Are you worried about scandal? Is that what this is about?"

"Setting aside the fact that you deceived me and are now insulting me to my face?"

"Well, I certainly would never insult you behind your back, my lord—you have my word on that. But yes, why don't we set those two things aside for a moment?"

Jeremy took another breath.

"Scandal is a catching thing. It rubs off on people around you." His voice lowered. "It leaves one's progeny tainted." His cousins were proof enough of that. But his cousins weren't at the forefront of his mind. Begetting his heir, however, was.

Eliza's cheeks darkened. "I don't believe this is the appropriate time to discuss—to discuss *progeny*, my lord."

"Don't you?"

Her eyes narrowed on him. "You're trying to intimidate me, my lord. Just like you did in those horrid letters. It's not going to work. I've lived with a bully since the moment I was born, and I am not about to allow you to do to me what my mother did."

Jeremy almost stumbled backward. "I am *nothing* like Lady Rushworth."

"You have a strange way of showing it."

The conversation was slipping from his control. "Nobody speaks to me like this."

She crossed her arm below her breasts. The dog yapped at

him. "It's clearly time somebody did."

She exhaled and squared her shoulders. "I think I should return to the house to allow you some time—"

"We'll discuss it now."

"What is there left to discuss, my lord?" She waved a hand helplessly through the air. "What's done is done."

He stepped toward her, and the little dog gave him a warning yap to approach no closer to its mistress. Jeremy ignored the creature. "I don't think there is an ecclesiastical court in the world that would deny me an annulment."

She frowned at him. "You're not going to seek an annulment."

"No?"

"No. You're so averse to scandal, you won't put one foot wrong, even if the repercussions of an annulment would be far greater for me than for you."

"Then where does that leave us, do you suppose?"

"I'm prepared to be a good wife to you, my lord."

The sentiment only encouraged his imagination to take another turn through explicit and lurid scenes of what exactly being a good wife would entail. Sitting on his cock and riding him in wild abandon until they were both rendered boneless in the aftermath of intense pleasure, for example.

"Are you now?" He couldn't help himself. He knew what he thought a good wife should do. He had to hear what she thought. "And what do you suppose that entails?"

"I'll be a good partner to you, you can depend upon it. I'm levelheaded. I never succumb to hysterics. I'll go to *any* length to protect the ones I love. And I don't remain silent in the face of wrongdoing."

"And you suppose that is what I need, is it?" Jeremy didn't much care for the insinuation that marrying Christiana could have been considered a wrongdoing. Because, unfortunately, Eliza was all too correct. It would have been wrong. Instead of standing up to Lady Rushworth himself, he'd been all too ready to ruin a young woman's life. He'd needed Eliza to stand up against him and show him he'd abandoned sense.

The fact remained, however, that she had deceived him. He'd married the wrong woman. Like she'd so aptly pointed out, he wasn't about to seek an annulment. He'd bring no hint of scandal upon himself or his family. Ever. Not for *any* reason.

So they were stuck with each other.

"What else could you possibly need?"

"If you must know, only one thing comes to mind."

"One thing?" She shook her head, frowning as if he were speaking in riddles she couldn't puzzle out. "What's that?"

"An heir."

Chapter Twelve

Trembling, Eliza shut herself into her room and threw herself onto the bed, tugging carefully tucked covers over herself until she was safe inside a tight cocoon. She'd been bluffing when she'd told him she didn't think he'd seek an annulment. Testing him, really.

She had fully intended to tell him *everything*, but when the moment had come, she'd been unable to speak. Speaking would have made it real. Speaking would have brought back all those memories that she thought time had slowly let drift into unimportance.

Foolish. Foolish. Foolish. It was of *utmost* importance. And now, apparently, the only thing the earl claimed to want from her was an heir.

Of course, she'd known it would come to this. In the orangery, she'd faced her husband like the woman she wanted to be. Strong. Unwilling to apologize for having done what was required to save Christiana.

She squeezed her eyes shut as Captain Pearson's words once again battered her brain. *Whore.* Would she ever be free of his ghost? Not if she was about to live the debacle over again with Lord Bennington. The thought turned her stomach. She kicked her way free of the covers, took Daisy in her arms, and went to where she'd hidden the jewels. They were still her way out.

She'd no sooner turned the key in the lock than Christiana all but waltzed into the room. Her eyes were bright, her hair in some disarray. After the incident with the lambs and the ruined carriage, however, it was hardly noticeable.

"Daisy," Christiana all but purred, pulling the dog into her lap on its back and rubbing the exposed belly. "If there are more in the litter to be had, I want one, too."

Eliza tried to smile, but inside she was hollow. Her reserves had ebbed away. "Of course. I'll let the earl know."

As she finally focused on her cousin, Christiana's features drew into concern. "Is everything quite all right?"

"Oh, my dear. Please don't worry about me."

There was a pause. "You told him, didn't you?"

Eliza gave half of a nod.

Christiana's breath caught. "And?"

"I wish I knew." Eliza slipped the key to the jewel box into the dressing table and slid the door shut. "I can't stop myself from feeling that I've let him down."

"Let him down? But he couldn't have had any *expectation* of you. Not yet."

Expectation? No expectation, indeed. Only an heir. He might despise her, but that wouldn't prevent him from bedding her.

Eliza's throat nearly closed, and she struggled to seem as normal as possible as she continued the conversation in a casual tone. "Of course, people have expectations of one another. Fair or not, that's human nature. But I think in his case, it was entirely fair of him to expect that the woman he thought he married not drag him into unexpected scandal."

"What scandal? You're a lady. He's a lord. You had one broken engagement, not ideal, certainly, but it can't be as bad as all *that*, can it?"

"I deceived him into marrying the wrong woman." *Deceived.* That was the word the earl had used. It sounded so coarse. So wicked and so unlike her. Yet it was precisely what she had done. "If that's not the stuff scandals are made of…"

"Who has to know? I can't imagine your mother wanting to bring the scandal down upon herself, so no matter how displeased she is, she won't say anything."

Eliza held her tongue. There was always the risk that her past would come back to haunt her. But not the part of her past that Christiana knew about. If anyone ever learned the details of where and how she'd surrendered her virginity, it would be scandal of the highest degree. And there was always the risk, wasn't there? Because the man who'd taken it from her had but to whisper a word in the right ear, and the gossip would be all around Society by the end of the week.

Christiana spoke gently. "So what have you decided?"

"I haven't decided anything." Eliza straightened, unable to bear another moment of the torturous conversation. "But he tells me Tom has come. Is this true?"

Christiana colored prettily. "We're to be married tomorrow."

"On your birthday. How perfect. He has the special license?"

Neither of the parties having resided at Idlewood long enough to qualify for a common license, they'd need the special license. Tom had pined for Christiana from almost the moment he'd first laid eyes upon her. No doubt it hadn't taken him long to begin plotting how he'd make her his bride, especially after she had given him a resounding no when he'd posed the question of elopement.

"He does." She pushed to standing, and, right there in the

middle of the ornate bedchamber, she swirled, clasping her hands together in delight. "I can't believe it's finally going to happen."

It was so like Tom to be aware of the technicalities such as marriage licensing requirements. Christiana was going to be well matched with such an excellent man.

An unfamiliar sensation prickled behind Eliza's eyes, hot and strange. "I'm so terribly happy for you, cousin. You deserve this."

And Christiana did. She had the biggest heart of anyone Eliza had ever known. Nobody was more deserving of happiness with the man she loved. Eliza would never regret giving her the chance to make the marriage she'd been born to make.

Never.

Chapter Thirteen

In the morning, Jeremy stood beside Eliza in a shaft of light coming through the stained-glass windows in the dank church witnessing Miss Burke and Lieutenant Hart pledge themselves to each other for eternity.

It was difficult not to witness two people coming together out of real affection and ignore the strange sensation that he'd been too hasty and too final in his judgment against love matches. Making his own was an option that was closed to him, though. Forever.

He'd never thought he'd make one himself, true enough, even before Lady Rushworth had taken the choice from his hands. Then Eliza had schemed to marry him when he was supposed to have been marrying Christiana. He should have known something was amiss when the two of them arrived early and without Lady Rushworth. He'd been too blinded by Eliza's beauty to think of anything else but what it was going to be like when he took her to bed.

It wasn't the first time being randy as a goat in spring had gotten him into trouble. But it far and away eclipsed every other unfortunate incident, in both magnitude and repercussions. All the more reason to redouble his efforts to keep his urges in check. He knew well enough how powerful his needs were. He *must* maintain the control to remain master over them.

He stared at Christiana. She was certainly pretty. Young, though. Far too young, really. What was she, all of twenty-one? She wasn't a silly girl, he could say that, but he couldn't dream of ever having anything to say to her. Moreover, he couldn't picture himself being intimate with her. The idea alone made his delicate areas clench with the wrongness of it.

It wasn't supposed to be like this. One unmarried woman of good reputation and standing should have been interchangeable with any other. He wasn't supposed to feel any hint of possessiveness toward his wife, no matter who she was. Least of all toward the one who'd deceived him in such a heinous manner.

The clergyman began the final blessing, and Jeremy bowed his head. A church was not the time and place for vengeful thoughts.

"I pronounce you man and wife."

Lieutenant and Mrs. Hart beamed at one another. The lieutenant gave his bride a knowing look that made her gaze fall to the ground and her cheeks fill with color. Light glinted off Christiana's spectacles.

Witnessing the bond between them flung Jeremy square into the middle of a place he did *not* want to be. Suddenly, he was all too aware of the woman by his side. His wife. The woman who'd deceived him into marrying her when he'd promised to marry another.

Outside, as they led the informal procession down a narrow dirt path to Idlewood, Jeremy went back and forth with himself about whether or not he should speak. These notions were as new and unfamiliar as they were unexpected.

"You said in the orangery that you'd wished the letters had worked." When he'd rehearsed the question in his head, there'd been no vulnerability. Reality was far different. As he was standing beside her, there was a small measure of…well, exposure. He had to rally his gumption to continue and pray that he concealed more than he revealed. "Is that true?"

Eliza didn't hesitate. "You can't expect me to rejoice in this marriage, can you, my lord? I might have schemed my way into it, but it was born of desperation."

They were walking side by side, her arm in his, as if they were a real couple. But they were strangers to each other. No. Worse than strangers. Because they had this wretched thing between them.

"Are you telling me that you don't care to be married to me any more than I care to be married to you?"

"I suppose. But unlike you, my lord, I'm prepared to make the best of it."

"There is nothing out of which we can make the best. The situation is entirely hopeless. We can't recover from where we started. I don't suggest we try, because I can never forgive you."

The words were harsh for so beautiful a day. The sun was warm, the brilliant sky all the bluer for the high white clouds scattered here and there. Birds twittered, and the occasional red squirrel bounded up a tree trunk in hasty pursuit of who knew what.

"If you'd approached inheriting the title with that attitude, you'd never have gotten to where you are today."

"That's entirely different." Was it? Or did he only want it to be? For ten years he'd had nobody to vent his anger over what his uncle had done. Now he had this. Was he punishing her beyond reason?

No. She'd *tricked him into marriage*.

"But you forget, my lord, that I never asked your

forgiveness. Perhaps I should be the one telling you to beg mine."

Never let it be said his wife didn't have a backbone. "That's outrageous."

They walked a little longer in silence. It irked that she didn't think highly of him. It shouldn't have, but it did. He didn't want to care about the opinion of others, but even he couldn't be blind to the fact that he'd spent the last ten years of his life single-mindedly bent on restoring the family reputation, at any cost.

"I've been thinking about the orangery."

Jeremy glanced down at her. "What?"

She paused in the shade of a young oak and turned in the direction of the dilapidated old building. It stood on the far edge of the gardens, the ruin out of place among the careful cultivation about to hit the peak of the season. "Why do you think it's unnecessary?"

"I had to make choices. The orangery isn't good for much that's important in day-to-day life."

The others made their way into the house. Eliza, seemingly unaware or uncaring that they were alone, frowned, still looking across the gardens. "Perhaps it's time you began to rebuild."

"The plans are in the works. I had to deliberate for a while before I decided to do so, however. I didn't know if it meant anything. But it'll complete the picture, and that's what's important."

"That's what's important? How things look?"

"How things look is of the utmost importance. The rest is nothing more than diversions, and I don't have time for diversions."

"Maybe that's why you're perpetually in a sour mood, my lord."

"If my mood has been sour of late, my lady, you might

think of what role you played in the matter."

She arched her brows at him. "Whatever mood you do or do not find yourself in, my lord, is entirely your own affair."

"You must take some responsibility—"

"For your moods? No. None. None at all. They're your business and your concern. If I made it my life's work to please those around me, I'd die raving in an asylum. Now, for my actions, I can take full responsibility." She turned serious, and her voice lowered. "I always have, and I always will."

The air between them was suddenly tense. Jeremy studied her a long moment. If only he could peer into her and see what had caused her to speak in such a way. It was as if she were haunted by something. As if somewhere in her past she'd gone horribly wrong and she still hadn't forgiven herself.

Of course. It must be related to what went wrong between her and her former fiancé.

Jeremy muttered a curse below his breath. Damn him if a fierce burden of protectiveness hadn't fallen upon his shoulders. He couldn't help himself. She *was* his wife, however they'd gone about it, and if anyone had tried to crush her vibrant soul…

He had to take a deep breath. He was trembling from unchecked rage. The urges toward violence could be so strong—almost unbearably so.

Suddenly she was the one studying him. "Are you quite well, my lord?"

She reached out to take his hand, warmth swirling in his veins at the unanticipated intimacy.

"Nothing more than too much coffee at breakfast, I'm sure."

"You like your coffee, don't you? At least you have that."

"What's that supposed to mean?"

"I mean you've got nothing in your life that you really *live* for."

The pronouncement rankled. "I've worked—"

"Yes, I know." She waved. "You have much to be proud of, my lord, that I would never dispute. But the only thing you do is work."

"That's the only thing for which I've had any time."

"That's the only thing for which you've *given* yourself any time. You treat life like it's a game of subterfuge."

"I suppose I'll take your word for that one, my lady. Since you're the resident expert on subterfuge."

She colored.

They went on in silence. His shoulders ached from tension.

"I used to play the violin." Lord save him. He didn't need to tell her this—he hadn't spoken of it in years. He had nothing to prove. Whatever she thought of him…he didn't care.

"You did?"

He scowled and sighed. "I started lessons when I was a lad. And I hated them—every last second. I finally wore my mother down and finagled her help in convincing my father to let me abandon music all together. It wasn't easy. My father was…a difficult man."

Eliza's eyes were full of tender concern. She said nothing. Only waited.

Jeremy looked away and continued. "No sooner had I put down the instrument—forever, I'd thought—than I longed to pick it up again. After a year, I could stand it no longer, and demanded to resume lessons. But on my own terms and with a new master."

That's when they'd found Mr. Oswald, a man with a deep passion for music instead of a deep passion for petty punishments.

With Eliza's hand over his, Jeremy allowed himself to feel the full measure of the guilt he'd pushed away for years, telling himself it no longer mattered because the estate and the family name were more important than anything else.

He didn't want to let go, though—didn't want to admit that perhaps he'd taken things too far. He raised his chin and withdrew his hand. "Music is nothing more than a frivolity."

When she reached for him again, he pulled away.

"My lord…" Her was face full of concern, her voice soft. It would be so easy to kiss her now. To capture her lips with his and drink her long and deeply, inhaling the rosy scent of her. "I don't think those things are frivolous. Least of all music. You're entirely wrong on that score. Perhaps you should think about taking it up again."

"It's too late for that."

Chapter Fourteen

Eliza retired as late as she possibly could. With Tom in the house and the wedding festivities, she and Lord Bennington had not found any more time to talk. When they'd been forced to interact, they'd been stiff and formal with each other.

She lay under the covers in darkness so black, it didn't matter if she kept her eyes open or closed. Her hand rested upon Daisy's curled body, the dog having nestled against her hip.

Eliza bit her lower lip. The last thing she had ever wanted to do was confide her wretched shame to another human being. After Captain Pearson, she'd sworn she'd never speak of it again.

A frank conversation with a trusted friend after her marriage had left Eliza reasonably certain that men couldn't tell the state of a woman's virginity, for all the talk that purported otherwise. Although she'd toyed with the notion of not telling Lord Bennington, she owed him the truth.

Her insides churned with nausea at the thought of his reaction to her confession. The feeling between them was already tense and angry. Confessing her darkest secret was going to demolish any hope that life between them could ever become cordial. Once he knew—once he saw her for the defiled woman she was—he would hate her forever.

There was a tap on the door joining her chamber to his.

Her heart started pounding. Everything inside her wanted to turn over, pull the covers over her head, and stay perfectly still. He would think she'd fallen asleep and leave her in peace.

Coward. What would that solve?

A voice—hers, it seemed, although her nerves were far too frazzled to be certain—broke the silence. "Come in."

"My lady?"

"Yes?" She pushed herself up to sitting, pulling her knees close. Daisy ran to the end of the bed, then back up to nose into Eliza's lap.

The light from the candle illuminated the angles in his features. It was like he wore some wild and fantastical mask.

She still hadn't told him, and he was here to start the process of trying to conceive the heir he'd told her he wanted. What did she fear more—the conversation or the inevitable coupling? Maybe it would have been easier if he'd banished her from his sight upon news of the original deception.

Her hand wandered to her neck, remembering the weight of the stones. How connected she'd always felt to her father when she'd worn the jewels he'd given her. That wouldn't go away simply by selling the object—she could have taken a different path when she'd first learned of her mother's plan for Christiana. But the idea of parting with the jewels had always felt like trying to cut away a piece of herself.

She resorted to drawing on courage she didn't know if she actually possessed. "If it's an heir you want, you'd best be about it."

The moment the impetuous words were out of her mouth,

she regretted them. She owed him the truth about herself before they began their endeavor. The secret was a snake in the grass ready to bite.

"I think there are a few things we need to discuss."

Her heart began to pound. Provide him an heir and then quietly disappear into a dusty old corner of England and never bother him again. However, if he thought for one minute that she'd be surrendering a heir to him and vanishing from her own child's life… "All right."

It was a reprieve. As much as she didn't want to discuss anything further with this man, it kept her from having to tell him her sordid story. Then maybe he really would toss her out on her ear.

"First, forgive me for being indelicate, but I want to know if you married me because you're…er…" He cleared his throat. "Because you've gotten yourself with another man's child."

The question, too dangerously close to what she had to tell him about herself, made her stomach go hollow. "No. It was strictly because of Christiana."

There was a long silence. He stared at her, his face so like a garish mask in the candlelight. And completely unreadable.

Finally, Eliza ventured to speak again. "Do you believe me?"

Something shifted in his face. "In fact, I do. I don't know if I should. But I do."

"But?"

"I'm going to need an heir." The low notes of his voice brought an unholy awareness between her legs. A sort of… warmth. It was unusual, but rather nice.

She mentally started. Good Lord in heaven, she didn't actually want the earl to *bed* her, did she? A kiss was one thing. *That* was quite another. There might have been reason to believe that relations could actually be enjoyable for other women. Not for her—and certainly never with the man who resented her deception as deeply as he did. "We discussed this, my lord."

"Yes. Yes. I need you to know and understand something."

"And that is?"

"There can be no more scandal. Nothing. Not one more hint of anything untoward. I will not stand for it. I've worked too hard to restore honor to the family name and the title. I won't have anyone else sully me ever again, least of all someone as intimately connected with me as my wife."

Eliza had gone weak and dizzy under the weight of his pronouncement. Her throat was dry, and her voice emerged high and strange when she tried speaking. "Of course, I understand, my lord."

"If there is anything else I should know—anything at all—now would be the time to tell me."

It sounded for all the world as if he had something in mind. Was he purposefully giving her the opportunity to confess? No. That was impossible. Nobody knew.

The burden of her secret was going to crush her. She was cold suddenly with the renewed realization of just how alone she was. But what else had she expected?

"If you had something in mind, you'd best tell me what it is you think you ought to hear."

He was silent a moment. "Your mother, she…"

"Is this really the time to discuss *her*, my lord?"

"Now that I've put the question out there, you might as well answer it."

Eliza shrugged. "She would die before being involved in any scandal. As it is, I'm sure what I did is going to be impossible for her to accept. Now before we…uh…do the necessary business, I think you ought to know that I won't be leaving any child of mine."

"What are you talking about?"

"I'm not going to give you a son and then quietly bow out of your lives. I…" She'd meant to say that she'd always wanted to be a mother—except in those few harrowing weeks at fourteen when she'd come to understand the full measure of what she'd done—but her voice threatened to quaver, so she went in another direction. "I'm willing to be minimally involved in your life, because I know that is what you shall want, but I want to help raise my child."

"There is no question in my mind that it would be any other way, my lady."

"Good. Now are we going to get on with this heir business, or are you going to leave me in peace?"

It was a gamble—she sensed that if she pushed him, he'd leave, instead of coming to her bed. Then she could think about how to handle her confession another day. At a more appropriate time than when they were about to have relations.

Sure enough, the earl's lips flattened to a stern line. "Leave you in peace? Is that what you would prefer?"

"I'm perfectly willing to give you an heir, my lord. Never fear." At least that wasn't a lie. "I surrender myself completely to my duty."

"That's…precisely what I needed to hear." Was it her imagination, or did he sound as if he were fighting strangulation? He took a deep breath. The candle in his hands wavered. "On second though, it's been rather a hard—uh… that is, I think perhaps we can begin another day. Er, night. Sleep well, my lady."

Chapter Fifteen

The next morning, in the corner of a forgotten music room, Jeremy opened the violin case and stared inside, near choking with guilt. Untouched for a decade, the instrument was in some disrepair. A thousand memories flooded his brain as he inhaled the smell. The happier parts of his childhood, when he'd lost himself in music.

Mr. Oswald, his beloved master, had had little in the way of belongings, but upon his death, he'd willed Jeremy his prized violin.

"For my best student," he'd said on his deathbed, pale and fragile, when he'd handed the instrument over. A while later, he was gone. Jeremy would always be grateful for being able to see the man through his final hours. After Mr. Oswald's last breath, Jeremy had had the honor of shutting the man's eyes and arranging his hands. It had been a clear and strangely quiet day—one of the saddest and most beautiful of Jeremy's life. Mr. Oswald had been the father Jeremy's own sire had not been.

Truth be told, by measure of sheer talent, he hadn't been

Mr. Oswald's best student. For the pleasure Jeremy received from playing and his passion for the music, he'd outshone all the rest.

Jeremy had not done right by the man's memory. Used to be that he didn't think much about what he'd given up. Once in a while, he'd find himself running his left thumb over the pads of his fingers, absently feeling for calluses. He'd catch himself and resolve to do better in the future. To remember what he had to do and why he had to do it. To remember that playing the violin was an indulgence he could no longer afford.

It had all been about the name. The scandal. The estate. And, most importantly, that damn debt.

Eliza's face appeared in his mind's eye. The way she'd looked at him at the edge of the gardens after Miss Burke and Lieutenant Hart had married…

Without so much as reaching for the instrument, he shut the case, tucked it away, and checked the mantel clock. Not quite ten, and he'd neglected to have his coffee. Normally, he'd go to the breakfast room, but Eliza could be there. Or could appear at any moment. But he didn't want to call it up to his desk. It seemed so uncouth, and he hated the risk of knocking the cup over on his papers.

Having coffee was the one thing he did for himself every day. In light of the memories of his more musical days, it seemed all the more important that he not let the pleasure of his morning drink be pushed aside for business.

To hell with it. He could face his wife. There was no point in avoiding her, was there?

Jeremy had no more than stepped into the breakfast room than he instantly regretted his choice. The sight of Eliza at the table roused his base desires. He had no business being quite so *up*, as it were, at such a time.

The force of what surged through his bloodstream

should have frightened him. There was no reason for such a heightened state. He was accustomed to being levelheaded, of doing what needed to be done and leaving his personal feelings aside.

After returning to his own room last night and once again relieving the worst of his urges with a quick tug, he'd stared into the blackness for a full hour replaying the conversation in his mind to see where he'd gone wrong. That was three nights in a row he'd been ready to do the deed. Three nights in a row he'd come within steps of her bed. And three nights in a row, he'd slunk away before attending to the critical business. It was beginning to skirt all too closely to being a pattern.

He should've had done with it. It didn't need to be anything more than it was, so he told himself again. It was no more than a simple mechanism that all animals participated in when creating the next generation.

Inwardly, he cursed himself. He didn't really think that, and he wasn't going to convince himself of it. Not for a second. As much as he wanted to be cool and detached toward Eliza, he wasn't. She stirred him in ways he should have been able to withstand. He wanted things to be better between them. In bed, that was. Not just a quick *in and out and thank you very much, my lady, sleep well.* There had never been anything polite about it in any of his past endeavors. He didn't care to begin now.

Food. He needed to temporarily abandon this tangle of lewd thoughts and concentrate on the meal. He couldn't avoid her forever. At least not until their nocturnal activities produced the desired result. He was strong enough to not lose his mind over a stiff cock in the presence of a beautiful woman.

One thing was certain. Tonight when he came into her bedroom—assuming she was fully willing—he wouldn't leave before breaking this absurd barrier between them. So to speak.

Lieutenant and Mrs. Hart were not in evidence. Good for them. Jeremy hoped they were going at it like rabbits. Someone in the house should be enjoying carnal pleasures.

Eliza was frowning over a letter.

It didn't matter. He wasn't going to ask.

Was there enough business in the day to keep him distracted from his absurd yearning to bed her? He'd probably have to go back to his room briefly to have himself off. This was one of those times requiring extra help. "Where's the dog?"

"It turns out she's quite untrustworthy in the presence of food, so I had a footman take her outside to run about a bit." She folded the letter and put it aside.

"He, you mean."

She took a sip of tea. "I suppose so."

He had to tear his eyes away from her mouth. The shape her delicate pink lips took when she was about to place them on the china cup was more than he would be able to withstand. "I take it you haven't thought of a more suitable name."

Turning from fixing himself a plate, his eyes fell upon the graceful curve of his wife's neck as she sat with her back to him studying her letter. A few strands of her dark hair curled artfully over her nape. He tensed. That damn glorious hair. What was it about those glossy deep-brown depths that turned him helpless before a woman?

Helpless before *her*.

No. Never.

She folded her letter as he came around and put it away. "Nothing seems right."

With a plate full from his selections from the sideboard, he took a seat across from her. "How about Dash? Or…"

Was it his imagination, or did Eliza look pale?

Scowling, he took a breath. There was no need whatsoever

to make conversation. He stuffed his mouth with a rasher and washed it down with the smooth splendor of perfectly prepared coffee.

She was still frowning. It didn't sit well with him, her frowning. He didn't like it. And he didn't like that he didn't like it, either.

Hell and damnation, but he was curious. "Is anything amiss?"

Her hand came to rest over the letter. "This came a few minutes ago by urgent messenger."

"Bad news?"

"Yes. But I know what I'm going to do about it, because there is only one right thing."

It didn't take much effort to put the pieces together. "Saying that suggests you might be worried about my reaction."

"I am, my lord."

Which means Lady Rushworth is somehow involved. "Your mother?" *Say no.*

"She's ill, and she needs me."

An unwanted stab of jealousy pierced his heart. He didn't want to share her. Which was absurd, because he didn't want her—except in his bed, where he would make her the mother of his children—and, even if he did, she certainly didn't belong to him.

He kept his voice level and hoped he sounded aloof. "She's written to you?"

"She hasn't, no. It's our servant—Caruthers. He promised to care for my mother in my stead, and he told me she took the news of my marriage hard—and then she fell ill—"

Her expression irked him. It was like she expected him to forbid her. As if he were some sort of tyrant.

"I'm not going to forbid you anything. That way lies a person I don't want to become." The next words he spoke were as much for the dominant side of his nature raring to assert itself as they were for her. "You're my wife, not my prisoner."

If he sounded half as ridiculous as he felt, it would be too much. It didn't help matters one whit when her eyes widened.

Jeremy drew a deep breath, his whole being stinging with regret. His control was slipping. He slunk back to stiff formality. "I must own that I don't understand why you want to go."

"I don't expect you to. But I do expect you to support my decision."

"Give me some credit and at least attempt an explanation, won't you?"

"I want to be a good daughter."

He wanted to ask her how that interacted with being a good wife, but doing so would have been unpardonably selfish. The last thing he wanted to do was suggest that he was the reason for her existence. Men who treated their wives as property were vile. Jeremy would not join their ranks.

"Do you want to be the good daughter, or do you want to run away from your duty?" His jaw clenched. Control. He needed to maintain control—to keep his anger in check. He wasn't being careful enough.

Her color heightened. "I suppose you mean my duty to give you an heir."

Jeremy could have hung his head in shame for letting his tongue fly loose before thinking through his words. He was better than this. "I did, but I must beg you to forgive me. Don't answer my absurd question. Consider, however, that we have only just arrived at Idlewood."

What little he knew of Lady Rushworth was enough to make him lay heavy odds on this sudden illness of hers being nothing more than a fabrication devised to separate her daughter from her new husband.

Gathering the vestiges of control so he could see the conversation through with as much grace as possible, Jeremy remained silent a moment. He took a deep breath. Whatever guilt she struggled with over having married him was not his to dismiss, absolve, or deny. "I won't ask anything of you. What you do is, and always will be, entirely up to you."

Her wide eyes were grave. "I have to return to London to be with her."

"Does she live in London the year round?"

"She doesn't like my cousin who inherited my father's title and refuses the dower house because it's too close to him." Eliza nodded. "Margaret will be glad of going. She's been homesick, I think, although she hasn't said anything."

"Homesick? Haven't my servants been welcoming to her?"

"Oh, I don't think that's the issue. It's different for her, is all."

"Very well." Jeremy started for the door. "I shall alert the servants, we can be on the road by—"

"Oh, you don't have to go to such trouble for me."

He froze, not having entertained the possibility of her going without him with any seriousness. Slowly, he turned. "I'm sorry?"

"I mean, you don't have to come. I'm not sure she would want it."

It took him a few extra moments to find the right words. How carefully should he tread around the subject of her mother when their relationship was still so new? "She spent a lot of your life controlling you, didn't she?"

"She did her best to try." Eliza bowed her head—whether because she was abashed or because she didn't like the reminder, it was impossible to tell. "But she is my mother, and I have dishonored her by going so far against her wishes. You might think me foolish, but I do earnestly want her forgiveness."

A rush of tenderness took him by surprise. How could he think her foolish for having such a heart as that?

"You do?"

He must have sounded more surprised than he'd meant to, for Eliza returned with a flash of resolve that wedged in a tender place in his heart. "She's my mother."

Ignoring whatever he might have been feeling, he pushed the point. He needed a sense of how she viewed her mother. "Do you think perhaps this sudden illness of hers might be a way of trying to reassert control?"

Giving a little shrug, she took another sip of tea. "It could be. She's capable of such things."

Those were the exact words he needed to hear. He exhaled a released breath. For her to be at least somewhat aware of her mother's shortcomings, to put it lightly, boded well. He shouldn't have doubted her. She was highly intelligent. But even the smartest people could have such blind spots.

Which meant for now, he'd relax. By the time they reached London, he'd have to brace for battle, if not an outright war. Lady Rushworth would not take kindly to his accompanying her daughter. If he guessed correctly, it would foil her plans.

Then again, she was not a woman to be underestimated. One point in his favor would likely neither be forgiven nor forgotten. "I'm coming."

Eliza set down her teacup and gave him a frank stare. "You don't have to protect me from her, you know. I've been alone with her for years. I know how to manage myself around her."

Something tugged at the back of his mind when she spoke of being alone. Like there were more to the statement than an offhand remark. He filed it away.

"I'm certain I don't." Like hell he didn't. Lady Rushworth was ruthless. Eliza was strong, but his instinct to protect her was too much to overrule. And just let the coldhearted shrew try sending him away.

"My lord, I think I understand your point of view." She spoke in a firm manner suggesting he might have been trying her patience. "However, you're the very last person my mother would have wanted me to marry. It will be better for all concerned if I return for the first time alone."

She possessed no small measure of quiet strength, his wife. It was exactly the sort of thing to make him weak-headed around her. It did not, however, abate his desire to protect her.

"Don't worry, my lord." She spoke as if reading his thoughts. "I withstood many years with my mother. And while I am eager to begin my own life, I can withstand a few more weeks."

"A few weeks?"

"As long as it takes to see her well again."

The thought of being so long without Eliza made a sensation ripple under his skin not unlike what an army of ants might have felt like.

The fact that he had such a visceral reaction to the mere idea of being without her said that maybe he should, in fact, be without her for a while. He needed distance. Time. Time to regain mastery over his control.

Chapter Sixteen

By one of the clock, Margaret had finished repacking their trunks. Half an hour later, Eliza was on the earl's arm as he led her over the gravel drive toward the carriage. From the outside, it must have looked as it ought to—a man seeing his wife off before she departed on a journey.

Her internal perspective was entirely different. Whenever he was close, it was difficult to stop thinking about those two times their lips had met. At some point or other, they'd have to do more.

Except it was all so complicated. Part of her wished the dastardly business was already over and done with forever. That he'd come to her, done what was required, and returned to his own room no later than five minutes after knocking on her door, leaving her pregnant and in peace.

Another part of her wished that her whole life could be different. That she'd never been ruined, that she'd never met Captain Pearson, and that somehow she and Lord Bennington had found each other in the ordinary way—at a ball or via an introduction from a mutual friend. There was something between them. An energy. An *attraction*. It could have really been something if it weren't for the sins that blackened her soul.

Her regrets had never been heavier than when he kissed her.

They stopped before the carriage. Margaret went in first. Eliza held out her hand to her husband, expecting stiff formality. Certainly nothing like the morning they'd married and he'd brushed his lips against hers in the street.

Abruptly, without speaking a word, he pulled her close, wrapping his arms around her. Their bodies pressed together. When their mouths met, it was with the force of determination. His determination. And more—he was angry with her, there was no question. The heat behind the kiss was at once helpless need and heady rage. It said, *you're mine, and this isn't over*.

Eliza went weak against him. Oh, yes, there was something between them. No doubt at all. It was strong and intoxicating. And that something would have to be reckoned with sooner or later.

The kiss ended as abruptly as it started. Before she knew what was happening, Eliza was shut inside the carriage with a yipping Daisy and Margaret, who, expression a little too innocent, was looking out the other window.

As soon as Eliza settled into her seat, Daisy happily in her lap, she plucked a stray clump of wool from the doorframe of the carriage. She was still breathless and shaking a little as the driver set the horses to trot.

The earl's coat of arms on the door was an odd contrast to the current state of the interior. The conveyance had been made serviceable enough for use, but required restoration.

She bit the side of her lip. Who would have known lambs could do this amount of damage?

As they rattled along the drive, Eliza stroked Daisy's silky ears, trying to banish that last kiss from her mind. At least

Christiana hadn't been there to witness it, leaving Eliza free from questions she couldn't answer. Tom had three weeks of leave from his regiment, two of which he was using to take his bride to Lyme Regis, that they might walk along the sea and collect fossils on the shoreline. As happy as Eliza was for her cousin, she would miss her terribly.

The window was empty of glass, allowing in the sweet breeze of the grasses and fields they passed. She leaned out, watching Idlewood grow smaller and smaller, until it vanished behind trees.

She hadn't been entirely truthful with her husband. Again. Her mother *was* sick. Caruthers had said she should come.

When Margaret nodded off, Eliza pulled out a second letter from her reticule—a letter from her oldest and dearest friend, Hetty. Hetty was Lady Henrietta, the young sister of the Earl of Corbeau. The earl was Lady Rushworth's godson and one of the few people who didn't cause the woman any displeasure…until he'd married Jeremy's cousin Lady Grace Landon, whose father had been the late Earl of Bennington.

Hetty wrote long missives, full of news and gossip. Several lines, however, had caught Eliza's notice, which she reread now for the dozenth time.

> *And then there is that odious Sir Domnall fellow who has ingratiated himself with Lady Tutsby. They're always together now, which means I don't often see her or Fredericka anymore. It's a loss to our musical endeavors, certainly, but I'd rather eat a rat than spend one minute in Sir Domnall's company.*

Lady Tutsby was a widow and a distracted mother, widely known to be eager to remarry before her daughter came out. And Miss Fredericka Chapman, Lady Tutsby's only child, was a fourteen-year-old girl on the brink of becoming a beauty.

Fourteen. The girl was *fourteen*.

It sent Eliza tumbling back through time. In her mouth, she could all but feel the texture of those tart cherries he'd brought her.

She gagged.

Sir Domnall was a name she didn't want to remember. He was the man from Eliza's past, and she'd thought she'd never see him again. But he'd returned, this time venturing into the heart of London Society. He thought he was safe. Quite probably, he had been.

The image of the man being near that willful, headstrong young girl, Fredericka, made Eliza's blood turn to ice. Because she alone knew what Sir Domnall was capable of doing, it fell upon her to stop him.

And stop him she would.

Upon arriving at her mother's house, Eliza realized she hadn't been away long enough. She scratched Daisy's ears to remind herself that her marriage had not been a dream.

Caruthers took her things, a soft warmth on his wizened old squinting face. "It's good to see you again, my lady."

She replied in an undertone. "How has she been?"

The butler took her cue and lowered his voice. "Not well. She's missed you. We all have. We're terribly happy for you, of course, and I don't feel disloyal admitting it, if you don't mind my saying."

"Happy" was a dangerous word, because it was something she wasn't entitled to have. Eliza might rejoice at being out of her mother's house, out from under the burden of her rule. But that didn't make what Eliza had done *right*.

She swallowed, looking down, a burst of hot shame threatening her composure.

If Lord Bennington were here, his strength would help keep hers within reach. But she'd spent so many years alone with her mother that it wouldn't do to become so completely dependent on another at this stage, would it?

The question didn't matter, because Lord Bennington was not here.

She forced her attention back to the matter at hand. "Thank you, Caruthers."

He cast a suspicious glance at Daisy. "Is she…expecting *that*, my lady?"

Daisy yipped, startling the butler. Eliza scratched the pup's ears. "Perhaps you ought to have a footman take her outside for a bit."

As she ascended, her heart unexpectedly started pounding.

Outside her mother's sitting room, she paused. Eliza drew in one final steadying breath before the inevitable happened. Maybe there was no right answer when it came to the problem of her mother. Nothing she could do would change the fact of their relation—a thought that had seen her through many days and nights wishing to be someone else living a completely different life.

Lady Rushworth was lying upon the chaise longue, bolstered by pillows and covered tidily in blankets. The room was warm and stuffy, and the air smelled faintly of bitter herbal tonics. A small table rested nearby, with various and sundry glasses, vials, and other sickroom items within arm's reach. Her face was sallow, her lips thin. Her cheeks appeared gray and hollow, and dark circles ringed her eyes. She clutched a handkerchief bordered in lace.

It appeared her illness had not been exaggerated.

"The prodigal child returns."

And so it began. Calling her prodigal was not fair, but Eliza was in no mood to point it out. If she opened the topic, her annoyance would have the better of her—and that was not what she wanted these first minutes with her mother to be. "Well, then, I shall look forward to dinner."

"What?"

"It's been so long since we've enjoyed fatted calf."

"Disgraceful." Lady Rushworth scowled, fussing with her coverings. "I suppose Christiana has married that *soldier*?"

She intoned the word "soldier" with more contempt than other people reserved for the muck that men wiped off the bottoms of their boots.

"He's a brave and honorable man, with several commendations from high-ranking officers. We should be proud he's now part of our family."

"That man is no part of any family of mine, any more than your husband is."

Eliza kept her voice dispassionate. It was important to stand up for herself. "You don't get to make that decision."

"Apparently not. But I should have. I'm your *mother*. How could you have done this to me? A *Landon*."

"I think even you would be in awe of all he's accomplished. Remember what I told you Grace said about the condition of the house when they were forced to leave it?" Come down to it, there was no point in arguing with Lady Rushworth. Still, Eliza couldn't help but feel it was important to her to maintain her resistance. "You would never dream she was talking about Idlewood, in the state it's in now."

Lady Rushworth waved a hand. "So he made a few prudent investments and can hire workmen. How is that supposed to impress me?"

"You were going to force him to marry Christiana."

Eliza studied her mother's reaction. Her mother knew about Christiana's true parentage. She knew, too, of course, but Lady Rushworth didn't know they shared the secret. For the first time, it struck Eliza that her mother must be a very lonely woman—alone and isolated in a cold world of her own making.

"That's entirely different. He's an earl. Any other girl would have been grateful to marry a distinguished man instead of a nobody."

Eliza shook her head. She did not understand why her mother chose to live in the grip of such anger and resentment.

Refreshments arrived, saving Eliza the trouble of saying anything else. She poured them both tea. Judging by the tray of food, it seemed Cook had anticipated her, having prepared all her favorites.

Perhaps later she would have more of an appetite.

Her mother spoke at last. "Aren't you going to ask how I've been?"

"I know how you've been. And I'm sorry I've been such a disappointment to you."

She'd spent a good deal of the journey to London debating whether she owed her mother any sort of apology for what she'd done. She'd been undecided on the matter, so it was a surprise when the words came forth anyway.

Lady Rushworth waved. "You're my daughter. And a beautiful woman, Eliza. You owe more to the world than to have married that derelict."

"That doesn't make the least bit of sense." As if by being beautiful she owed something to the world. Absurd.

"You weren't in your right mind. You'll get the marriage annulled." She spoke as if obtaining an annulment were as simple as buying ribbons on Bond Street.

"No." Her mother's words only redoubled Eliza's resolve. "That isn't going to happen, Mother."

Lady Rushworth narrowed her eyes. "Are you doing this to spite me, you ungrateful child?"

"In fact, I'm not."

"I don't believe you."

Eliza remained calm. With all she had yet to face with Lord Bennington, her mother's pettiness didn't ruffle her in the slightest. "I didn't think you would."

Chapter Seventeen

Eliza was sitting in the lesser drawing room with Hetty, catching up on all the London news. Hetty was all light and happiness, with a pleasingly plump figure. She made a becoming picture.

"Do you like being married?" Hetty took a sip of tea. She'd asked the question as if it were in the same category as asking if Eliza enjoyed London.

A crumb of Hetty's shortbread fell to the floor, which vanished immediately under Daisy's vigilance.

"It's difficult to say after so little time. Ask me again in a year."

"You waited long enough. Grace did, too, I know, but you hadn't any of her impediments." *Impediments* was a polite way of referring to being penniless and having a father soaked in infamy.

If Hetty knew what had kept Eliza from marrying… Warmth spread over her cheeks, and she busied herself with stroking her dog's ears. No, it was better nobody knew. She couldn't trust anyone with that part of her past.

Not even Hetty.

It was too easy to think herself safe. Too easy to think she had someone in whom to confide. Someone who would stand by her side. She'd made that mistake before. It had cost her dearly.

She was completely alone. Alone with her secret. Alone without a friend for company, despite appearances to the contrary, which was the very worst way to be alone.

The sensation of isolation was all the more acute now that she'd had a taste of a new life.

Daisy lost interest in waiting for another crumb and started chewing on the wooden foot of Hetty's chair. Eliza scooped her up before her tiny puppy teeth could do much damage. The dog rolled on her back and stretched out, giving Eliza a significant look that she'd come to know was the canine way of saying, "This is my belly—won't you be so good as to rub it gently?"

She smiled. At least she had Daisy.

Hetty's round cheeks went a shade pinker than usual. "You're going to keep them all guessing, aren't you?"

Eliza took a sip of her tea. "Keep all who guessing?"

"Oh, everyone," Hetty said. "First you shock everyone by clandestinely marrying a man your mother has made no secret of despising—"

"It wasn't a clandestine marriage." The protest felt weak. Strictly speaking, the marriage had been everything but.

Hetty ignored her. "Then you return to London—to your mother's house—after being gone with your new husband less than a week."

"My mother fell ill. She needs me." Eliza took another yeasty confection from the tray. "When is your next musical afternoon? I thought it might be nice to join you. That is, if you'll have me."

A musical afternoon would be a welcome reprieve. A

chance to be with her friends and make merry while enjoying the chance to sing and play.

"Oh, we'd love to have you." Hetty brightened. "I'll talk to my brother. It's one of the few things he actually likes to do with people outside the family—other than argue in Westminster—so we try to arrange them around his schedule."

"Is Miss Chapman still coming?" Eliza prayed her tone sounded as offhanded as she intended.

Hetty leaned back, shaking her head. "She hasn't come in a few weeks. It's such a shame. Her mother has taken up with this..." She made a face. "...*man*. None of us like him. Well, like I told you in my letter, *I* don't like him. Grace is indifferent, and my brother has no patience for him but doesn't think much else one way or another. And Lady Tutsby is making such a fool of herself over him. I'm inclined to think him some sort of magician who's put a spell on her. I can't imagine he's up to any good. And that he denies us Fredericka's presence makes me despise him more."

Eliza bit into her cake, the crumb dry and tasteless in her mouth.

Somehow she would keep the young girl from the old lecher's clutches. What had happened to Eliza would *not* happen to Fredericka.

Chapter Eighteen

Jeremy scanned the ballroom. "You promised me she'd be here."

Grace swatted him on the arm with her fan. "Patience, cousin. Really, one would think…well, I don't know what one would think, but this behavior is baffling, to say the least."

He ground his teeth together. The past few days without Eliza had been impossibly long. Since she'd left, he'd seen her in his dreams every night, but she was walking away and couldn't hear him calling her back. He'd wake up in a confused panic, his mood thoroughly fouled by the sense of being out of control while he slept.

He scanned the room again. And saw her.

No sooner had he fixed his gaze upon her than the smile faded from her lips and her head turned. Their eyes met. A charge of energy shot through Jeremy, renewing him in his purpose. It was like there was something greater than anything else drawing them helplessly to each other.

He was all too ready to surrender. He'd never imagined a wife might have such power over him. If someone had suggested as much, he might have turned in revulsion at the thought.

But what was between them was anything but revolting.

Why must there be so many people here tonight? So many bodies stood between them, heedless of his need to be near her. A decidedly nonsensical part of him sparked in annoyance at the crowd, as if each person there were individually responsible for keeping him away from Lady Bennington.

Grace tapped him with her fan again. "I daresay I'm of no more use here."

"What?" He blinked himself back into the present moment. "I'll see you later, cousin."

Almost too impatient to allow himself to finish the farewell, Jeremy began cutting through the groups of people, barely nodding to acquaintances as he went. For himself, he could endure being thought rude. Reparations could be made later—a realization as unanticipated as it was absurdly freeing.

The closer he came to her, the harder his heart began beating. It was a wild and untamed pulse, with the speed and rush that nearly matched the glow of euphoria after the most vigorous lovemaking.

She was aware of him—he could tell. She looked this way and that, trying to concentrate on her companions in the little group in which she stood.

But there was something about her concentrated expression, like she was trying much too hard *not* to look his way that suggested her mind was full of nothing but him.

It was a powerful feeling. One to which he could readily become accustomed.

As he was almost upon her at last, she touched her hair with self-conscious awareness.

And then a man appeared before Eliza. He had a mop

of dark-golden curls and a smile Jeremy would have liked to remove by force. Great force.

Without the least awareness that he wasn't wanted, the man bowed before Eliza and reached out his hand.

Possessiveness flooded Jeremy's senses. It was unlike anything he could ever have imagined. *Mine.* It was all he could do not to stalk to Eliza's side and shove the man away. She was his wife. Nobody else could, or would ever, have any claim on her.

What happened next played out in painfully slow detail, as though Jeremy were in a dream where he couldn't move fast enough to prevent the disaster he saw coming. The curly-haired man was reaching for Eliza.

"I believe I have her for this dance, my good sir." The golden-haired man shot Jeremy a ruthless scowl.

Jeremy's teeth clenched. Hard. Didn't this insolent pup know who he was?

And the unthinkable happened. She began to reach for the golden-haired man.

Before her hand met the other man's, she sent a sidelong glance to Jeremy and blinked once, the message in her eyes as clear as if she'd spoken in a silent room. *I'm sorry*, she'd said.

And she took the other man's arm. Together they turned, their backs to Jeremy as he stood helpless as the pair went to take their positions in the dance.

He could have choked on the injustice of it. She didn't belong with anybody else.

Perhaps ten years of all but completely ignoring his own personal preferences had caught up with him at last. Pretending he didn't have wants of his own, of living for no more than his name, his property, and his legacy—they'd all come to a head here and now in the sharp intensity of his want for *her*.

At a ball, of all places.

As little as two weeks ago, it would have been impossible to imagine his life coming to this. Here now, however, with the people moving about him, with the dance beginning and Eliza the partner of another man, it was impossible to imagine his life any other way.

• • •

Eliza did her best to conceal the landscape of her inner feelings from her dance partner. All she wanted to do was go to her husband. But she had an obligation to the person whose arm she held. Sir Harold Alcott was a fine man, always in a good humor and quick with his easy smiles. He was a friend, and an awfully good one at that.

Early in their acquaintance, it'd been clear he'd thought of her romantically. When she'd signaled appropriately, he'd respected her gentle rebuff. He'd never shown the least resentment at her lack of interest.

Stepping through the dance, her skin warmed with the awareness of her husband watching from afar. His gaze glowed with banked fire, never moving from her since she had gone to the dance floor with Sir Harold.

Knowing the earl attended her…knowing he waited for her, too…her patience stretched to the very limit. Eliza went this way and that, working through the figures by rote. She kept a smile on her face and listened well enough to supply the correct responses at the appropriate times.

"You're distracted."

The dance had ended at last, and Sir Harold was walking her back to her group of friends.

She kept her eyes fixed forward. "Am I?"

"Well, I won't pry, my dear." Giving a knowing nod, he patted her hand. "You know that if you ever need anything, you can always come to me."

"Thank you, Sir Harold."

He gave one of his easy grins. "Will you forgive me if I tell you that you look more lovely than ever?"

"How kind of you to say so."

"Oh, it's not kindness. No, nothing of the sort. I'm afraid I'm rather ruthless in these matters, you see. And I have a very discerning eye."

He teased, of course.

She caught Lord Bennington staring at her, and her breath caught. She looked away. "Have I ever told you how much I value our friendship…how much I value you as a friend?"

"Never you worry on that score." Sir Harold spoke with mock sincerity. "I'm well aware of my many merits…there now, I've coaxed a smile from you at last. My evening is complete."

Lord Bennington appeared before them. Sir Harold sized up the earl, his eyes narrowing in unspoken challenge—an expression Eliza had never seen cross his ever-affable features.

Whatever did these two men see in each other that put them at such odds?

Lord Bennington responded in kind, his voice cold as a Scottish mountain peak when he spoke. "Lady Bennington, would you do me the great honor of going somewhere where we might speak in private?"

"You don't have to go with him, Eliza."

"It's quite all right." She turned to her friend, the awareness of Lord Bennington's closeness all too acute to be at ease. The best she could hope was to remain cool and allow herself time to think before speaking. "He's my husband."

Sir Harold's mouth fell open. "*This* is the man you married?" He glanced between Eliza and the earl, looking like he didn't want to believe it.

"Indeed."

Calm came over her as she took the earl's escort.

A few glances came their way as they wound through the other guests. Her cheeks warmed a little. They were making a spectacle of themselves—and more than simply by being together in Society as husband and wife. Everyone had to know about their marriage by now. And everyone had to know she'd returned to London alone. Now they also knew that the earl had come after her. How that was going to set tongues wagging.

Chapter Nineteen

So what if they were drawing stares? Jeremy didn't care if it wasn't the done thing for a married couple to acknowledge each other's existence in a social setting. Surprisingly, he didn't care what these people thought they knew of their affairs. What they believed didn't matter.

At least, not to him. A wife complicated the equation.

Her hair had been parted in the middle, and two featherlight ringlets framed her face. The simplicity set off the symphonic arrangement of her beauty.

Having Eliza on his arm drew up an unexpected welling of warm gratification. It was hard not to think that having her made him the most fortunate man in the room…that she was his *wife* made him the most fortunate man in the world.

"I want to go someplace private where we can have a quiet word."

A few rooms away from the ballroom was a gallery. The house boasted a magnificent art collection, the mistress of the place being renowned for her taste. Her husband, by all accounts, knew comically little about his wife's passion, though he was happy enough for her to spend what money she pleased, and he boasted prodigiously of her prowess.

The world beyond the windows was cloaked in black, but in the gallery, a dozen or so candles on three freestanding candelabra lit the room. The room was otherwise deserted.

Jeremy wouldn't have been able to trust himself had he taken Eliza to a more secluded spot. He was desperate to toss up her skirts and take her hard and fast…or even slowly and tenderly, stroking her and caressing her. Just so long as he could have her.

Neither of them spoke until they were standing in the far end of the long space before one of those horrid paintings of bountiful abundance. Innumerable fruits and vegetables were crowded on the canvas in a great heap, their depiction precise but not the least bit appetizing. So far as he knew, that could have been the point.

Eliza's features were calm and collected, but her voice betrayed a hint of tension. "What are you doing here?"

"My man of business called me here on an urgent matter."

"What matter is that?"

"I haven't seen him yet." Because Jeremy's desire to see her first had outweighed everything else.

"What did you want to talk to me about?"

Talk to her about? He wanted to be near her. He wanted to touch her and taste her, to see that glorious dark hair down about her shoulders. He hadn't known how much until she'd gone.

"You *deceived* me." It wasn't what he meant to say. It was what had mistakenly emerged. Because it all came back to that, didn't it?

"Which I have owned several times over." She sighed. "I'm growing weary of this conversation, my lord. Either forgive me or not, that's your business."

"It will always be between us." No matter how much he

might want her, he could never forget what she'd done.

"Is that your final pronouncement, my lord?"

"It is."

"And what am I supposed to say to that, exactly? If you don't want to move on, that's also your business, but pray keep your boorishness to yourself when we're together."

Jeremy's passions flared to life. With a few long strides, he pinned her against the wall between two paintings, his arms on either side of hers, hands pressed flat against the plaster. "I'm boorish, am I? I have half a mind to show you exactly how *boorish* I want to be with you."

Her eyes were huge, her cheeks flushed. "My lord…"

"You have no idea how much I want to *bore* myself into you. To show you the depths of my anger toward you by bringing you to the very brink of pleasure again and again until you're begging me to allow you your release."

"That sounds cruel."

"It does, rather, doesn't it?"

"Are you a cruel man?"

"No more so than my desire for you has tortured me into my present state."

• • •

His desire for her? Eliza's cheeks went hot. The earl's dark scowl eased somewhat when he flicked a glance over her. One glance. That's all it took. The power and virility of his maleness brought to life an awareness of herself she hadn't realized existed until he'd come into her life. It was as frightening as it was exhilarating. Inappropriate thoughts intruded into the front of her mind. Ideas, images, and wants she'd hardly dared allow herself to have, after they'd led her to ruination.

"If you're angry at me because you"—it was difficult to force the word out—"*desire* me, then I suggest you go away and have a good long think until your blood cools."

"It's funny you say that because that's what I once thought. But I've come to realize it's not possible. My blood will never cool around you. I've regretted every moment since you left." His lips came close, and his voice dropped. "For having let you go without first taking you to my bed."

He could have kissed her again. Oh, dear sweet Lord, why wouldn't he kiss her? He smelled of those welcome days of early spring when the new season was in the air but not yet visible in the flora. It made her want to surrender to him in a way she'd sworn she'd never surrender to a man again. Why him? This interaction here and now only proved just how dangerous he was to her.

Fighting to maintain control of her hard-won sense, she gave him a little push. "You're hardly behaving appropriately."

"We're alone." His low voice melted her last reserves. He wanted her. Shockingly, she liked him wanting her. And more surprisingly, she wanted him, too.

"We're at a ball. Someone could come in at any moment."

"It's hardly going to ruin us. We're married."

"My lord, you told me very plainly that there was to be no scandal. You're as responsible for maintaining that scandal-free ideal as I am."

"Don't I know it only too well." He ran his fingers through his hair.

In her peripheral vision, she caught sight of a couple entering the gallery. Which meant they were no longer alone, dash it all.

Eliza, pulling away from her husband now that others were present, was about to reply when a laugh from her nightmares clawed icy nails down the whole distance of her spine. She went numb.

He was here.

She winced.

And, sure enough, as she helplessly turned toward the source of the sound, there he was.

Sir Domnall.

She clasped her hand over her mouth so she wouldn't retch. If he came close enough for her to catch a hint of that particular fragrance he'd worn the summer she'd known him, she would lose the contents of her stomach all over the gallery floor.

Lord Bennington grabbed her elbow before she even knew her legs were going weak.

He scowled. "You're ill. You need a doctor."

"No." She was stronger than this. She shook her head, trying to smile. "It's nothing. Too much canary wine earlier, I daresay."

"The devil it was. You haven't touched a drop of anything harder than lemonade, have you?"

"Don't you dare impugn my word." She was rattled by Sir Domnall's presence and taking her fright out on the wrong man.

"Don't lie and I won't have to."

"No gentleman I know would ever say such a thing to a lady."

"I am a gentleman, and you are a lady." His teeth clenched. "You also happen to be *my wife*."

"What do you know of me?"

His countenance went dark. "Less than I would like, it would seem. There is a wall between us. Is there something you need to tell me?"

"Of course not." Eliza swallowed. The lie was supposed to protect her, and it would, but it also compounded her sins. Her cheeks radiated that horrible, stinging warmth—the badge of shame for the untruth.

"Whatever secrets you're keeping from me, wife, I'm going to have them out of you."

Quite without her realizing, he was steering her toward the front of the house. They left the gallery and found their way to the entrance hall, where he told the servants to gather their things.

He was so big. So strong. And so close. He couldn't possibly know what a comfort his presence was to her…how much she wanted to lean into him and allow him to be strong on her behalf. In all the years since that fateful summer, she'd never been able to rely on anybody else. She'd been so alone. She still was, even with him. Her secret once again become a desolate prison where, utterly alone, she awaited her true punishment.

"I can't leave now—not like this." She spoke in a whisper, unsure whether Sir Domnall had seen her, and praying he had not. "You said you wanted to stave off gossip, and here you are—"

"Yes, but you're unwell, and you're my wife, *Lady Bennington*. I'm going to take care of you."

Eliza had to ignore the velvety way he intoned her new title or be in danger of throwing herself directly into his arms and begging him to kiss her. And what a mortifying scene *that* would have been. "But people will talk."

"I don't wish to downplay the significance of the venom Society is more than willing to sip and share, but even I have my priorities, my lady."

The footman signaled to them, indicating their carriage was ready.

"We can't go without taking leave of our hosts."

"I'll write them a note."

"I know you took some time away from Society, my lord, but one doesn't simply leave this way and then—"

"They'll understand or they won't. My concern is for you." He tucked her hand around his elbow and led her out into the night.

"If you think you need to protect *me*—"

"Of course I need to protect you."

The hardness of his voice made Eliza simultaneously shiver with renewed awareness of how close together they were and made her want to balk against him. "I think of all the ladies in London, I'm one of the very last who'd need anything by way of protection, my lord."

"Are you now?"

Carriages cluttered the street. Coachmen stood in groups talking or sat around a makeshift table under a streetlight with cards. A few were attending horses, and still others worked a rag over the polished doors to ensure they didn't lose their gleam.

Then Lord Bennington was helping her into a carriage. He climbed in, took the bench seat opposite, and the door shut.

Panic leaped within her. Sir Domnall's ghost still hung over her like a demon on her shoulder threatening to tear everything away from her at a moment's notice.

The space inside was so small. And it was only the two of them, her and her husband—together and alone.

The window was still broken, so she didn't need to let down the glass. She opened her cape so the air of the late-spring night cooled the skin above the low neckline of her bodice.

The earl gave her a stern appraisal, far more than the situation merited. But he was still trying to puzzle something out, wasn't he? "What are you doing?"

"I'm overly warm, is all. Where are you taking me?"

"To your mother's, of course."

When they came to her mother's house, he helped her down and came with her to the door. "It's all right, my lord. You can go now. I'm quite safe."

"Go?" He scowled darkly. "Where am I to go, pray tell?"

Her pulse picked up pace. "To...wherever it is you are

staying, of course."

"I'm staying with *you*."

The heir. He wanted to begin working on conceiving the heir.

A panicked flutter erupted in the pit of her belly. "But, my mother—"

"She either gets you with me or she doesn't get you at all. It's as simple as that."

"No, actually, I don't think it is. I have a say in this, and I say…" She was cut off from finishing her thought by the butler opening the door to them.

Trembling with anticipation of the measure of her transgression, she stepped inside. Daisy ran down the stairs and leaped at her skirts. She scooped the sweet little pup into her arms.

Eliza had known Caruthers for the whole of her life. The last time the man had lost his squint, the head footman had spilled bright-red wine on the tablecloth in front of her mother.

That had been a decade and several head footmen ago.

With Lord Bennington standing outside the door, Caruthers opened his eyes wide enough to reveal his irises were a light golden brown.

The earl followed her inside, and the butler shut the door behind them.

A minute ago she hadn't wanted the earl to stay. All it took was stepping inside for her decision to be made. They were married. They could stay together—and where they pleased. Eliza wasn't going to tiptoe around Lady Rushworth's moods and whims any longer.

"Caruthers, have a room made up for his lordship, please." Eliza's insides were jelly. Her mother was going to have a fit. It was going to be awful. Lady Rushworth hated the Landons with every last fiber of her being. "The room next to mine."

Chapter Twenty

Instead of retiring directly, Eliza insisted they pay her mother a visit. "She'll be expecting me. And it'll be far better if she finds out you're staying here tonight than if she hears it from a servant, after the fact."

Having handed over their things to the footman while awkwardly juggling the dog from one hand to the other, they took the stairs up to the sitting room.

"This is where she spends her days recovering." Eliza spoke in a low voice outside the closed door. The cut of her high-waisted, opalescent gown skimming her figure just so. "Her physician recommended Bath, but she refused to go."

Of course she had.

"Oh, Nancy." Eliza caught the attention of a passing housemaid on her way up the stairs.

"Yes, my lady?"

"I think today isn't the day we let on to my mother that we've allowed a dog in the house. Have a footman take her into the garden. It's been a while, and we don't want any accidents overnight. And have the tea things sent up, won't you?"

"Tea, my lady?" The maid raised her brows.

"Yes, please. Tea."

Nancy nodded, took Daisy, and retraced her steps down the stairs.

"Tea?" Jeremy arched his brows in question once the maid had vanished.

"Medicinal."

"Wouldn't you care for something a bit stronger?" That wouldn't have gone amiss with Jeremy, but she let the comment pass without responding, instead staring at the door as if the oak panel would save her from whatever was coming next.

Without her animal companion, Eliza looked as if she didn't know what to do with her hands or arms. They hung stiffly by her sides, her shoulders straight, her neck long, and her hands alternating between fists and stretching her fingers long.

Without thinking, he reached out and slipped his hand around hers. "You're not alone."

She looked taken aback. "Why would you say such a thing?"

Although the impulse surprised him as much as it surprised her—maybe more—he wasn't going to back down. A protective instinct had surfaced. One he couldn't ignore.

He knew Lady Rushworth's ways well enough not to wish the woman's wrath on anyone. Eliza had withstood her mother alone for years. Now she had him. "Because you look as if you feel alone."

With her free hand, she cupped her check. "I do?"

"You have an ally in this, my lady. Me."

It was there no more than an instant, but it burned into his mind—the flash in her features of warmth and gratitude and strength. He'd put it there, he was sure of it. And if he died remembering the expression, he'd leave this world a happy man.

"But how can we be allies? I deceived you."

"I know. And, as I told you, that's going to be between us forever. But in this, you have me."

Head high, cheeks white, Eliza swept into the room, Jeremy following.

The last time he'd seen Lady Rushworth, she'd been blackmailing him into marrying Christiana. She'd played on the one thing he'd wanted the most in the world—to be free of that godforsaken debt his uncle had left him—and manipulated him into doing her bidding.

Lady Rushworth appeared to have aged ten years in the few days since he'd last seen her. She appeared shrunken, the wrinkles on her once handsome face cutting deeper and more harshly into the papery texture of her skin.

At the sight of him, her brows rose almost as high as her hairline. Just as quickly, the shock vanished. Her eyes narrowed. "That man is not allowed in my house."

Without replying, Eliza took the seat opposite, indicating to him that he should take the one beside her. The air in the room was thick with tension. Tea arrived, and none too soon.

"I'm not taking tea with him."

Ignoring her, Eliza took her mother's key and opened the box on the mantel where the dried leaves were kept. She moved through the ordinary tasks of preparing and pouring, the procedure loud and unsettling in the terse silence, the china's clinks unnaturally jarring.

"He doesn't think he's staying here, does he?"

Before Jeremy could answer, Eliza replied, her tone level. "He's my husband, Mother."

"Under *my* roof? Disgraceful. I won't hear of it."

The disgust in her voice suggested she had something particular in mind about what it was she didn't want done under her roof. Well, she wasn't wrong about that. Jeremy had to take a hasty sip of tea lest it show on his face exactly what he would like to be doing with Eliza.

Lady Rushworth clutched at the fichu around her throat as if it were the one thing between her and the devil himself. "He can very well make other arrangements."

"It's far too late for that, Mother."

"That's no problem of ours, my girl."

"I'm afraid I must insist upon one thing, my lady." Jeremy met Lady Rushworth's stare with one of his own. "Do not discuss me as if I weren't in the room."

Lady Rushworth turned pointedly toward her daughter.

Drawing a slow breath, Eliza put her cup down in her saucer. "No, I think we shall either both be staying here or both be staying elsewhere."

Lady Rushworth's eyes narrowed. "*I need* you *here*."

Eliza remained straight and calm. "Then it's simple, isn't it? We shall both be staying."

The way she stood up to her mother, determined and resolute, was humbling. He should have known that first day they'd come to Idlewood when she'd executed that absurd plan to get the runaway lambs in the carriage. She took action, this one. She didn't stand by and wait to be saved—she wasn't some damsel in distress.

Which made what had happened at the ball all the more puzzling. What did it take to spook a woman like Eliza? What was she hiding?

Why was this woman still a cipher to him? It made his blood pound with desperation to crack her open like a closed shell and peer inside. If only it were that simple.

"No. Not him. Not under my roof. After what he's done to you…" Lady Rushworth gave Lord Bennington an icy glance. Her voice was brittle. "So far as I'm concerned, this man is the worst kind of traitor."

"Worst kind of traitor, my lady?" Jeremy took a sip of his tea and spoke breezily, as if they were conversing about nothing more important than the weather. "Even after taking into consideration the depth of your feeling, that seems like a gross overstatement."

Lady Rushworth made a look of disgust. "The Landon blood never fails to assert itself."

"I'm a Landon, too, now, Mother." Eliza refilled her tea.

"That's remedied easily enough." Lady Rushworth waved a hand, the gemstones crusting her fingers glinting in the light from the candles. "You will get an annulment. Or you will leave and I will never see you again."

Chapter Twenty-One

It was midmorning and they were on their way to see friends for an informal musical gathering. When Eliza had invited him along, Jeremy had wanted to say no, but instead it had come out as a yes. Damn his tongue.

Lady Rushworth's pronouncement had eaten at his insides all night long. He hadn't visited Eliza's room last night. Maybe that had been a mistake. It would have cemented things between them.

"There will be no annulment." Jeremy could barely unclench his teeth enough to free the words from his jaw. The carriage jostled as the wheel found a rut.

Eliza turned her attention from the window and gave him a blank look. "I'm sorry?"

"There will be no annulment."

"I never asked for one."

He'd been stewing all night over his first meeting with Lady Rushworth since his marriage. It didn't simply sit uncomfortably with him. The idea of an annulment had been clawing at his insides. "Your mother—"

"—has no say in the matter."

"The last thing she said to you was that she never wanted to see you again. You were to leave and never return."

"I know. But she says things in anger sometimes, and..."

The way Eliza sighed tore his heart in two. Nobody should have to excuse such behavior of another person. That a mother could say such a thing to her daughter—her only child—and the daughter be so resigned. It wasn't right.

"It was a hell of a thing to say." He winced at the poor language that had slipped out.

"We *all* say or do things we regret." Her words were firm. "If we don't forgive, how can we expect forgiveness ourselves?"

Jeremy didn't like that logic—not for a moment. Oh, yes, it was exactly the sort of reasoning he aspired to himself. Except instead of merely *aspiring* to live by those words, as he did, Eliza actually seemed to embrace them without struggle. "That's not how I was raised."

"If I were to behave how I was raised, my lord..." Shaking her head, she laughed a knowing laugh. "Were you close to your father?"

The last thing he wanted to do was delve into that particular subject. Jeremy hedged. "I barely knew the man in any meaningful sense."

"I think of my father every day." A faraway look came to her eyes. Then a smile flashed over her face—bright and unstudied. The kind he rarely saw from her. "We had a game. For every time my mother said the word 'disgraceful' in our presence, he owed me a shilling."

"Sounds expensive."

"I still keep a mental tally in my head. And he's been gone..." She bowed her head, voice softening. "Such a long time. Sometimes it feels like he's been gone forever. Sometimes it feels like he might walk into the room at any moment."

There was a long silence.

At last, Eliza looked up. "Why do we have to lose the people we love?"

But they'd arrived, and that put an end to the conversation. He didn't know whether to be grateful or relieved. A few minutes later they were being shown into the music room at the Corbeau house in Mayfair.

The walls were creamy white, the ornate plaster ceiling high, and a few items of scrollwork were detailed in gold, though it had been treated with a restrained hand. Understated in the most elegant sort of way, subtly whispering to guests the reminder of the owner's wealth without the vulgarity of outright boastfulness.

Their hosts were the only people in evidence. Lord and Lady Corbeau, of course—the countess being Jeremy's cousin Grace. And Hetty.

Hetty's face brightened at the sight of them. "I'm delighted you could come today." She gave Jeremy a quick once-over. "Do you play or sing, my lord?"

"Neither with any degree of competency, I'm afraid."

Grace gave him a puzzled look. "You play the violin, don't you, cousin?"

"I haven't touched an instrument for years."

"No time like the present, though, is there?" Hetty beamed as she passed Jeremy a case.

He didn't reach for it. "Forgive me, my lady, I wouldn't dream of disappointing you, but couldn't possibly."

Then Eliza turned to him, her expression encouraging. "Pray do, my lord. I should like it very much."

Hetty smiled. "There. You can refuse me, but you can't very well refuse your wife, can you?"

For a fleeting second, he regretted having told Eliza about having once played. But the fact of the matter was—no, he most certainly could not refuse her. He took the instrument. It was as strange as it was wonderfully familiar. An old friend he hadn't realized he'd missed, having been too stupidly busy with matters he'd considered more important.

Strange. At the moment they didn't feel more important. In fact, he felt nothing if a little foolish for having abandoned everything he'd deemed superfluous in favor of things he'd thought deserved priority.

The last time he'd held one, he hadn't been an earl. He opened the lid to the scent of rosin and wood polish. The instrument gleamed. He hummed an A and plucked the strings, tuning by ear—no easy task, but one that his music master had spent hours training him to be able to do effectively.

It had been too long. He had no intention of playing before these people.

Regardless, he pulled out the bow and tightened the screw to make the horsehair taut. Then he rosined aggressively.

The mere act of touching one of the things that had provided so much happiness during his childhood brought an unexpected comfort. The smells he'd known so well, the feeling of the instrument in his hands. And it was a convenient distraction while he ignored the warm interactions among the other people in the room.

In the years since his resolution to rise above the scandal, he'd disdained Society. Now he saw how wrong he was. Oh, he might have been right about the stuffy balls and insipid conversation. But he'd done a disservice to a great number of people by assuming that there was no more than a single kind of person to be found.

Maybe it had been the lie he'd had to believe to remain focused on the task he'd set himself.

A force beyond him drew his gaze to Eliza. If he hadn't done everything he'd done, he might not have married her.

They might never have met.

Imagining a life without Eliza brought a hollow ache to the center of his chest.

Hetty let out a squeal of delight. "Fredericka!"

Corbeau's sister ran to greet the young girl who entered the room—a rosy creature with large eyes and fair hair. Hetty took the newcomer by the hand and brought her to the group. "I'm so pleased your mother allowed you to come today, for you can meet my very great friends"—she introduced the girl, Miss Fredericka Chapman, to Eliza and Jeremy in turn—"and they can have the pleasure of hearing you sing."

"My mother is coming, too, I'm afraid. She insisted. And *him*, of course." Fredericka gave Hetty a flat look and lifted her eyes to the ceiling, shaking her head.

"Never you mind about that. We're glad to see *you*. It's been too long." Hetty patted her friend's hand. She had a way about her of boosting everyone's spirits—quite an admirable woman. "Where are they?"

"If they found a crack in the earth and fell in, it would be—"

Two more people entered the room. With them, the mood shifted. Hetty's smile, a minute ago so bright, became stiff. Corbeau's stern look hardened, and Grace shot Fredericka a look of motherly concern.

The couple were introduced as Lady Tutsby, a slight woman with a crane's neck and a long nose, and Sir Domnall Gow, a distinguished gentlemen of some years, impeccably groomed, with an air of insincere graciousness.

But it was Eliza's reaction that put a shadow over Jeremy's mood.

Taking one look at her, Sir Domnall's mouth fell open. He recovered himself and dropped Lady Tutsby's arm to cross the room. Presumably to greet Eliza.

Eliza turned her back on the man and moved close to

Hetty and Fredericka, immediately engrossing them both in close conversation.

There was a quality to the paleness of her face that brought everything in his brain to a grinding halt as he stared, trying to discern what it was he saw. His Eliza was strong. Why did it look as if it took every ounce of willpower she could dredge from her veins to merely remain standing? What did it mean that her eyes had taken on so haunted a quality?

Something was terribly wrong.

Fear cut through Jeremy with the ease of a blade slitting the belly of a lamb. Icy rage burned in his veins. Jeremy would wager every scrap of respectability he'd fought, sweated, and bled to bring back to the Landon name that Sir Domnall—this smug, simpering, slippery excuse for a man—had a past with Eliza.

The very idea was too much. Instantly, his control began to slip. He stood on the edge of a dangerous precipice about to tumble forward—so close he was shaking.

It took a full five minutes before he was able to regain hold of himself.

Jeremy gently rested the violin on his chair and came to stand beside Grace. "How is Isabel?"

Grace smiled. "She's very well, I thank you. I take it you haven't yet been to see your mother since you've returned to London?"

Isabel was only nominally his mother's companion. Discovering her in a gaming hell had caught him completely unawares. He'd wanted her to leave—immediately—and she'd told him she had a duty to pay her father's debts to the house. That his uncle had had more debts than the acknowledged ones Jeremy was already paying—secret debts that his beautiful cousin was being forced to pay by working in that place… He had not taken the news well. They'd had a bit of a row over the business. One that, in the end, had accomplished nothing. She'd stayed, the stubborn woman.

"No, I haven't seen my mother yet." But now he needed her. If anyone could find out anything about Sir Domnall, it would be Isabel. Asking her would save him from having to hire a runner. "I will pay her a call tomorrow."

Chapter Twenty-Two

Eliza had to work unusually hard to concentrate on the afternoon's activities. Usually, music was a welcome reprieve from the harsh realities of the world. In this particular instance, however, it was a strain. Sir Domnall was too near. And Lord Bennington seemed to suspect something. Or was it her guilty conscious making her fancy seeing things that weren't there?

All she had to do was glance over to Fredericka, and her determination to see this through won out over her desire to run away from the newly opened wounds of her shameful past. She knew what Sir Domnall was capable of—and she would keep it that way. Fredericka should never have to endure what Eliza had.

Studying the girl was like stepping back in time for a view of what she herself had been like, once upon a time. The headstrong opinions, the vivacity, the fierce determination that nobody would see beyond the hard exterior to the inner confusion and hurt.

However, there was a critical difference. The summer Eliza had been fourteen, she'd been alone. She'd wanted to invite friends to stay with them, but she'd been too ashamed of her parents. She hadn't wanted anybody to know how they behaved like angry, willful children.

Then what she'd done had spiraled her more deeply into shame—a different kind. One that stripped her of critical pieces of herself, transforming her into a sullen creature.

That could *not* happen to Fredericka. The girl wasn't alone in the danger she would never know existed.

Climbing into the carriage, the full weight from the strain of the afternoon was upon Eliza's shoulders. They were stiff and tight, as if she were sixty-two instead of six and twenty.

"I wasn't aware you had such a beautiful soprano, my lady."

"I've always enjoyed singing." Eliza focused on her husband. The day was dimming, and the enclosed carriage cast his face into shadow. "But you didn't play for us."

"I...thought about it. But I'm afraid it's too late for me to take up music again."

She started. "Forgive me, my lord, but that's an absurd thing to say. If that was your philosophy, Idlewood would still lie in ruin. You turned it around in a mere ten years."

He waved a hand. "I had no choice."

"You gave yourself no choice. There is an enormous difference."

For a minute, it seemed as if he would argue with her. Then he relaxed, his eyes searching her face for something she couldn't perceive. "You're right, of course."

They continued in silence for a spell. Abruptly, the earl intruded on the quiet calm of the sound of the carriage wheels over the Mayfair streets. "Did something upset you this afternoon?"

He *had* noticed. She'd have to work harder at hiding her inner feelings. "Of course not."

Her conscience prickled at the lie. But it was for the best.

For the best…something she'd told herself for a long time about any number of things. For the best that she stayed with her mother. For the best that she was alone with her secret. For the best that she hadn't married Captain Pearson—although in that case, it absolutely had been for the best.

"Are you prone to melancholy, my lady?"

"No. Not at all."

"I wouldn't blame you if you were, you know. There is no shame in it."

She tilted her head at him. "That's an odd thing to say."

He paused. "My mother"—his voice went raspy—"she, well, for a long time…I mean there are some…I mean, I don't see it as a character flaw. It's foolish for anyone to believe otherwise."

He stared out the window, expression intensely concentrated.

Eliza wanted to reach for him. There was something tender in that difficult and complicated exterior. She knew all too well the pain of isolation. Lord Bennington was a great many things. A man without a heart, he was certainly not. Under different circumstances, she might have wanted to believe there was hope of her being able to carve out a small niche for herself inside that heart.

It could never be. Women with the stain of a sin as heinous as the one that sullied her didn't get second chances.

• • •

The following morning, at about the time his mother usually had finished her letters and descended to take breakfast, Jeremy rapped on her door and was shown in.

There was something about sharing the first meal of the day that Jeremy particularly liked. It was an intimate setting, yet relaxed. And people were generally in better spirits when there was food to be had.

His mother, Mrs. Landon, was indeed in the breakfast room, reading a newspaper over a light meal of bread and jam. Beside her, Isabel gave him a cool nod. His cousin was possessed of the sort of will that could have bent steel. By day she was no more than his mother's companion, and very seldom, if ever, in company. By night, she was the famed Beauty of Faro.

"Fix yourself a plate, my love." He leaned down to his mother, and she stretched her neck to meet him as he placed a kiss on her cheek. "Have you heard from Arthur lately?"

No matter what, no matter where, Arthur was always the first topic of conversation. Jeremy didn't resent the attention. His brother had given his mother pain from about the time he'd turned fifteen or sixteen. In a way, she grieved.

At the sideboard, Jeremy fixed himself a plate, not asking if she'd seen her younger son when their time in Bath overlapped, because he already suspected the answer was no.

"He came to the wedding." Jeremy sat. "He's tolerably well, I suppose. You know how he is."

"Yes, I know." That drew a sad sigh. She always said approximately the same things about her second son. "Poor lost boy. I do hope he finds his way. He was such a happy child. I would give anything to help him, but he has to want it first, doesn't he?"

"I couldn't agree more."

Mrs. Landon's cool hand reached out to pat his, and she gave him a wistful smile. It was as if she was acknowledging everything between them that neither could say.

Then she peered at his plate with open disapproval. "Is that all you're going to have? Only meat?"

"It's what I like. And no. It's not all I'm going to have." At precisely that moment, a footman set coffee before Jeremy. He raised the china cup in a little toast to his mother. She *tsked* and, shaking her head, went back to her own food.

The comfortable familiarity was still something he cherished. Growing up, he'd never thought to achieve this. Never considered it, really. He'd thought her fragile. Broken. It was still painful to think about, even so many years later, as the tightening in his chest reminded him.

When his father died, she'd mourned appropriately. Then she'd blossomed to life. He swallowed, saying a swift prayer that he—Jeremy—wouldn't do to Eliza what his father had done to his mother. It was paramount he remained in control.

"How was Bath?"

"Oh, you know. Bath." His mother shrugged. "When do you suppose would be the right time for me to pay a visit to your bride?"

"I'd quite forgotten you hadn't met her yet. That will have to be remedied." His mother and Eliza were going to get along like jam on cake.

Isabel excused herself. Jeremy spent a good hour with his mother before going to seek out his cousin. He found her in the lesser drawing room, the one that his mother had dedicated to all the things she loved without care of fashion or elegance. It was not quite the thing, such a room, but his mother had never cared.

On the wall were pictures he and Arthur had drawn as children. Other sundry items decorated the room. Little things they'd collected from traveling to this place or that. Things that helped her remember times she'd been happy, she said.

"I need to talk to you."

Isabel gave him an arch look. "If you think you have anything to say to me *this* time that will change my mind—"

"Actually, I want to know if you know anything about a particular person."

She sat back in her chair, but she didn't relax. Her eyes shone with a sort of ruthless intelligence that said very plainly no person—especially no male—should underestimate her. "I know a lot of things about a lot of people."

By contrast, few people knew about Isabel. His mother, of course. She'd known since the beginning, not sanctioning the arrangement—so she claimed—as much as giving Isabel a safe place to do something she was not going to be stopped from doing. Apparently, Isabel's youngest sister, Phoebe, had found out. And somehow, so had Phoebe's now husband, Max. Jeremy didn't have the whole story, and he wasn't sure he wanted it. Knowing would undoubtedly make him worry after his cousin's safety.

"What about a man named Sir Domnall Gow?"

She considered a moment. "A distinct name. I've heard it, I believe."

Jeremy frowned, perfectly prepared to play any game Isabel wished for information. "What will it take for you to know something about the man?"

If Isabel could have given him a sharper look, she'd have drawn blood. "That's not what I mean, cousin. What I mean is, I have heard the name. I don't know anything else. He must not come into Abraham's place. But I can, if you wish, try to find out."

Abraham. Ire heated Jeremy's blood at the casual way she mentioned the Christian name of the man who'd enslaved her. If Jeremy ever met the man, his control would be sorely tested indeed.

"Would you?" Considering the strength of the clash they'd experienced when he'd first discovered her double life, it was rather surprising she'd offer anything to the likes of him.

"Consider it an olive branch. Grace is always going on about needing to forgive and move on. I suppose I can practice her philosophy on you. See how it feels."

Jeremy cracked a small smile at her lightly teasing tone. "I appreciate it, cousin."

"Also, I assume it must be important for you to have come to me."

"It is important." The expression on Eliza's face when Sir Domnall had entered that room would haunt Jeremy to his grave. "Very important."

Chapter Twenty-Three

That night, Jeremy once again found himself on the other side of his wife's door. That he was in Lady Rushworth's house drew some compunction against knocking, but not enough to stop him. Fully aware of a husband and wife's right to make love when and where they pleased—observing the basic rules of decency, of course—he rapped lightly.

When the answer came, anticipation kicked his heart up a notch.

The room was smaller than expected. Or maybe it was that there were fewer candles lit than there ought to have been, drawing the shadows inward.

At the dressing table, his wife sat.

It was quiet and intimate. They were alone in her bedroom, and she was going to prepare for bed. *Bed.* Where he would join her.

"I—" He picked up the dog, who'd scampered up to him, and then addressed his wife. "You look tired."

"Not precisely a compliment, my lord." Eliza rose, still wearing the pale-pink gown she'd donned for dinner. It made him think of the morning in the orangery, and the little buds about to bloom on the bush that had grown wild with neglect.

The pup squirmed and whined, wiggling to free himself of Jeremy's grasp and return to his mistress.

"Here, Daisy." Eliza extracted the little dog, who strained upward with all its might until it was close enough to lick her chin. His wife laughed and pulled away.

"You haven't found another name, have you?"

She held the dog out to study him. "Everything about her says Daisy to me."

Daisy's tail wagged, and his tongue lolled happily as he panted. Eliza righted one of the silky ears that had gone amiss.

Who was Jeremy to say that the dog wasn't a Daisy? The little brown-and-white creature didn't seem distressed by the name. Nor by the incorrect pronoun, either.

"If he doesn't mind, who am I to mind for him?"

A smile tugged on Eliza's lips. "There. You see, Daisy? He might not understand, but he isn't unreasonable. What a good man your papa is."

The word jolted Jeremy down to the tips of his toes. Daisy, however, was looking at Jeremy as if he…she…he were phenomenally underwhelmed by the prospect of having Jeremy for anything.

Papa. Lord in heaven, Jeremy wanted an heir, sure enough, but he'd always thought of himself as *Father*. Stern and distant, and, most importantly, uninvolved. Papa, though, threw a whole slew of images before his eyes—children in his arms. Laughter. Eliza by his side, glowing with love and pride in their offspring.

His body was quite ready to begin making that scenario a reality immediately.

The part of him that still held firm in the court of rational thinking fought against the notion of impregnating Eliza too early. He'd have to share her with a child soon enough. For now, she was his. Maybe they could have a couple of—no, a trio of daughters before they had a boy. That would necessitate keeping her close.

"What's this?" Jeremy picked up the book left open on the bedside table, eyes going over words he hadn't thought about since Oxford. It was the New Testament. But not in English. "You read Greek?"

"Mmm." She nodded. "My mother wanted me to read Scripture every day. After I'd gone through once, I didn't want to go through again. My father helped us strike a compromise to reengage me with the material. He had some trouble finding a tutor who would agree to teach me, but he did. Now I continue, so I can keep in practice. I'm not very good, I must own. I only muddle through, but it amuses me. I prefer the original words to translations."

He took his wife's hands, pressing her fingers to his lips. In his semiaroused state, he had to tread carefully. Lovemaking in the early evening hours might shock her. She wasn't like the ready and willing women he'd taken to bed before he married. Eliza was a lady.

Lord help him, she'd turned him into a bumbling fool. Their marriage was supposed to have been about convenience—in so far as he and she were ever supposed to have been married to begin with. That aside, he would like to enjoy the intimate side of their relationship. He'd like her to enjoy it just as much.

Whatever had happened at the ball the other night and then at Lord Corbeau's—there would be time enough to delve into that later. Heedless of anything else, he pulled her closer and pressed his lips against hers. The scent of crushed rose petals made his blood run all the hotter.

Against him, Eliza froze.

He stood back, looking away and stinging with shame for being unable to control himself. "Forgive me, my lady."

She turned away. Head bent, she occupied herself by

neatening the arrangement of the items atop the dressing table. Her cheeks had bloomed with a dark-red stain. "There's nothing to forgive, I'm sure."

"Around you I—well, I can't make excuses for myself, so I won't."

She bit her lip. "I don't mind knowing what you think."

"It's not about what I think." He ran his fingers through his hair. His voice was gravelly—full of need enough to betray him to any woman slightly more experienced in worldly matters than his wife. "It's how I feel around you."

"And how is that, pray tell?" She still wasn't looking at him.

"Please don't make me tell you."

"Are you afraid?"

Afraid? What sort of man would he be to admit to such a feeling? Then again, what sort of man would he be if he didn't?

"I am rather. Yes."

"Of what?"

"Of frightening you, my lady."

She slid her gaze to him then. Their eyes met. Heat rushed downward, tightening his lower belly. "It's just…well, we're still dressed and…"

Then the door opened. Margaret's eyes went as big as two hardboiled eggs.

"Oh…" Eliza waved offhandedly. "I don't think it will be necessary tonight. I can manage for myself."

Margaret's gaze remained fixed on her young mistress, but Jeremy would have sworn he caught a flicker of understanding go through her features.

Eliza couldn't have missed it, either, for her whole face went red. "That will do, Margaret, thank you."

The maid held out a box. "This came for you just now, my lady. Messenger said it was urgent."

The rustle of Eliza's skirts seemed abnormally loud as she crossed the room.

A tremor of jealousy upset Jeremy's equilibrium. "From an admirer?"

She took the parcel from her maid and turned to shrug at him. "I haven't the first idea. Margaret, was there a note?"

"None, my lady."

Jeremy found a penknife in his pocket and offered it to Eliza. At the dressing table, she slipped the blade under the twine and the string fell away. Inside the box was a basket of some of the most beautiful cherries Jeremy had ever seen.

Eliza stepped backward with a gasp, hand to her throat. The penknife clattered on the floor. She'd gone pale.

Before he could ask what could be so upsetting about a basket of cherries, she'd thrust the box into Margaret's waiting arms. "I need you to find pigs."

The maid blinked at her mistress. "Pigs, my lady?"

"What the devil is this about, Eliza?"

She ignored him. "Yes, Margaret, pigs. I want you to pour these into the pen and watch them devour every last one. Can you do that?"

The little woman nodded, expression fraught with concern. "Of course, my lady."

"Oh, I know, it seems a terrible waste. But don't eat a single one. I'll buy you all the fruit you could possibly wish for. Just make sure that you don't eat a single one of these. Do you understand?"

The maid gave her promise and disappeared, shutting the door behind her. Silence fell over the room.

Eliza pressed her hand to her head. She still hadn't looked at him.

"I think it's time you told me exactly what is going on."

Chapter Twenty-Four

The time had come. Eliza could hide no longer.

They couldn't put off consummating the union forever. He wanted an heir. She was his wife. That's what lords and ladies did. They brought new people into the world to act as stewards to money and property. It was an odd thing, when one thought about it.

Not that it mattered now. She was about to lay herself bare. The small measure of something between them that seemed to have taken root would be obliterated forever. He'd hate her. She'd be more exposed than ever, but completely alone.

Lord Bennington's expression was dark. "What is so distressing about a basket of cherries that you direct your maid to feed them to *pigs*?"

"I hate cherries." Her voice emerged far more wobbly than she'd have liked. It was difficult to keep the onslaught of emotions from spilling over. "But I didn't always."

He stepped closer.

Part of her wished she could throw herself in his arms and

let him stroke her while she cried tears she hadn't let fall for more than a decade. Another part of her wished he'd locked the door before kissing her and that she had melted against him instead of turning to stone. If only telling him about her lack of virginity wasn't the right thing to do.

He'd despise her forever.

She took Daisy into her arms and stroked the silky ears. At least she had her dog.

"If your former fiancé used you and tossed you aside…" He spoke gently, though it seemed he had to exert great effort to do so. His tone would be so different when he knew.

Eliza shook her head. "It's worse, I'm afraid."

His mouth set, and he looked grim. His eyes darkened as he sighed, as if she was about to delve into the unthinkable. "I'm already imagining the worst."

"I don't think you are. Because when I tell you, you'll be shocked. I'm sorry for trapping you with me. For behaving so dishonorably—"

"And you think this is worse, do you?"

Her face stung, and her stomach was hollow. "About the worst thing possible."

"The worst thing possible is betrayal. I don't think we've been married long enough for you to have had any indiscretions."

"Please, my lord. Stop talking. This is terribly difficult. I know I must tell you, and you're not making it any easier."

His mouth set in a resigned line. "Very well. If you're ready."

She'd never be ready.

With a deep breath, she began. At the beginning. The last place she ever wanted her memories to return. "The summer I was fourteen, my parents were fighting. They almost completely ignored me. I thought I'd become invisible to them, and I hated them for the animosity and hostility and for not hiding it well enough in front of the servants and for forgetting about me. We were in the country, and I was left almost entirely to my own devices. And I met a man. An older man…who, well, he was—that is, I thought he was kind. I thought he liked me."

"He forced himself— "

"No." The memory tore at her insides. "It was nothing like that. It was worse. I wanted to…well, he treated me in this way that…I can't describe it. I felt like I was the center of his world and he told me…" The story wasn't coming together. She could only hang her head, burning with the hellfire of her acute shame. "I was lonely. I thought I loved him, and I thought that's what people who loved each other did."

Maybe what she'd done—what she'd allowed herself to do—had been in no small part because she'd wanted to hurt her parents.

What a price she'd had to pay for her rank stupidity.

There was a silent interlude in which it appeared for all the world as if Lord Bennington would turn and leave. Which would make everything so much worse.

"He was that man with Lady Tutsby at Lord Corbeau's house, wasn't he? And you saw him that night—at the ball—didn't you?"

She gave a small nod. "Yes."

"And the cherries? A present to win you back?"

"No. I'm far too old for him now." She shook her head. "It was a warning."

"A warning?"

"To keep silent. And to stay away. That if I try to tell anyone, he'll ruin me all over again."

Lord Bennington's face finally flushed with the anger she'd been expecting. She braced herself for the ugly words to come.

When he did speak, it was from between clenched teeth.

The jeweled depths of his eyes burned with blue fire. "I'll gut the rutting bastard."

• • •

Jeremy shook with unspent rage. It was the closest he'd ever felt to being ready to commit murder. That place in the center of his chest that he preferred to be completely numb instead wept with anguish for the girl who'd been hurt by a monster.

A thousand years of burning in the fiery pits of hell wouldn't begin to punish the bastard for what he'd done to her. The thought of that man holding power over Eliza any longer—no matter how tenuous—made Jeremy want to take the man by the throat and squeeze until he heard the bones of his neck crack. It should have frightened him, the force of just how much he wanted another human being to suffer.

Back in his school days, Jeremy had been disgusted with that old Greek hero Achilles, for black anger Jeremy couldn't comprehend. He'd hated *The Iliad* and had annoyed tutors and Oxford dons alike with his outspoken disdain. The man ought to have controlled himself better. So Jeremy had always thought.

What a fool he'd been. He'd been too young, too inexperienced to comprehend. Finally, he understood what it was to feel real anger.

In the bloodred haze of fury, he wanted to demand every last detail from her. What had happened? Would she ever be able to—well, not love again, for that was foolish. He wouldn't wish that upon her, not when he could never return the feeling. Love meant loss of control. That he could never risk. His uncle's compulsion to return to the card table night after night, gambling away everything, loving and hating what he did while wanting to stop and never having the strength to do so—that was lesson enough.

Jeremy was awash with helplessness, which only complicated and intensified the tempest of emotions in which he'd been caught.

In the mix with everything else was the vague awareness that the sin of her deception had diminished. Overtaken him was the sensation that she was his wife. His. Wife. And someone had hurt her in one of the most heinous ways possible.

His stomach dropped. That night at the ball—he'd behaved horribly. "It's not all right."

She paled, and her gaze fell to the floor. Her voice came out soft and shaky. "I know, my lord. I know. And I'm so sorry that—"

"You have nothing to be sorry for. *Nothing.*"

Her eyes widened on him. "What?"

He paced close to her. "What that vile gutter scum did to you…that sin is his, my lady."

"If only that were true. But it's not. I am to blame. At least partially."

"You were fourteen." How could he make her see? That she had carried the blame for so many years renewed his rage. That she saw herself at all culpable in it—that made everything far, far worse. Jeremy didn't just want to kill the man who'd done this to her. He wanted to make the bastard *suffer*. "He preyed upon you. He saw your tender heart and your loneliness and he twisted it for his own…"

Jeremy couldn't finish the thought. That there were such evil men in the world made him hate his entire gender, which wasn't right or fair. But he wasn't interested in being either. What had happened to Eliza wasn't right or fair. The world wasn't right or fair. Why should he bother?

"I suppose you don't want an heir from the likes of me now, do you?"

"How can you say that? Haven't you been listening to

what I've said? *It wasn't your fault.*"

"How can you not hate me for what I did?" Her voice was small. "I'm not…pure for you. You can't possibly want a woman like me to be the mother of your children."

Quite the contrary. "You're going to have to believe me when I tell you that I couldn't care less about the state of your virginity. You could have been with a regiment. I wouldn't care, so long as you are faithful to me now."

In body *and* mind.

A piece of the puzzle that was Eliza slipped into place in his head. Something he'd overheard about her flashed in his mind… "It's why your previous engagement came to an end, isn't it?"

She bowed her head and gave a slight nod. "I thought—I thought because he loved me…"

"He didn't love you. I'm sorry if that's painful for you to hear, but that's the truth of the matter. I know nothing about the subject of love myself—except that. Upon hearing a story like yours from a woman he loves, no man of any character would cast her aside."

For the briefest of moments, her lip wobbled, and her face flashed with the heartache she must have been feeling. Witnessing it cut Jeremy to the core. "Do you still love him?"

If she said yes, Jeremy didn't know what he'd do. Even the possibility that she did stirred a possessive rush of jealousy. She was *his*.

"Captain Pearson? Oh, good gracious, no. I haven't for many years."

Jeremy let out a breath. That was something, at least. It was bad enough that there was one man he wanted to kill.

There was an awkward pause. What was he supposed to do with himself now? "I suppose I ought to allow you to get some sleep."

"Oh." Her mouth opened and closed as if she were

searching for words. "I thought maybe...well, I mean"—her next words came out in a rush—"you still want an heir, don't you, my lord?"

The heir. The damn heir. He was instantly half hard in a needy rush of blood. His cock had had quite enough, and half begged for the satisfaction of finally sliding between her legs.

His voice came out in a strangled growl. "Of course."

"We need to get it over with."

Get it over with. Just what every man wanted to hear from a beautiful woman at the prospect of being taken into her bed.

But he was beyond being able to say no. Tonight, the last step in solidifying their marriage would be complete.

"I'll just...go behind the screen and make myself ready, shall I?"

He took the opportunity to go back to his room and remove his clothing. When he returned in his banyan, all the candles except one had been extinguished. Eliza sat on the side of the bed, knees tightly together, hands in her lap twisting around each other. Her hair was still up, which was a pity.

Jeremy cast Daisy a glance. All things considered, he didn't much fancy the notion of being in flagrante delicto with his wife while the dog supervised the affair. And in flagrante delicto with Eliza was precisely where he would end up.

Chapter Twenty-Five

Eliza's cheeks burned, and her pulse beat wildly. The one thing she'd thought she'd never do again—it was going to happen. Heaven help her. It was going to happen. And with *him*.

Just when she was about to try to say something, the earl took Daisy in his arms, shutting her in the other room. "Can't very well manage it with a dog watching the proceedings, can we?" Then he came to the side of the bed and pinched out the candle.

At the closed door, Daisy whined and scratched.

In the darkness, there was the sound of fabric fluttering to the floor. His banyan falling away, no doubt.

Which meant…

Oh, Lord. He was nude.

Eliza went warm, a delicious tightness pulling between her legs. It was unexpected, this, but welcome. He was, after all, quite the specimen of a man—with self-assurance, power, and that ineffable quality of maleness that made her remember she was a sinner.

"Lie down."

She worked herself down on the bed until she was flat on the mattress. Her breath was coming shallow and hard.

The two times she'd done this before had been painful. The first time, he'd tried being gentle with her and said he understood when she'd cried. The second time, though, he had said it was her fault he was angry—her tears provoked him, he'd said—and he'd hurt her. Which had caused her to cry harder. She'd felt so foolish. So childish. So alone.

There had been no third time.

He'd tried to tell her that it was too late. That she couldn't say no after saying yes. But her mother had returned to London suddenly, taking Eliza with her. That had been the end of it.

She squeezed her eyes shut, desperate for the old memories to evaporate into nothing. Lord Bennington was a different man. When they did this, it wouldn't be fornication. They were married and had the church's authority to be together.

Although thinking about it in those terms didn't increase the appeal of the task. It rather made it feel like leathery old men would be peering in and nodding their approval.

Lord Bennington eased himself down, pushing up her shift and brushing her bare thigh as he went. The air was cool on her skin.

He ran his hand down her body, his touch gentle. Reverent. Which was altogether lovelier than expected. A simple caress shouldn't have done this to her—made her want *more*. Want things she didn't know she was capable of wanting. It all came back to him. To how it was going to be: *his* body with hers.

But then he stopped. She wanted to tell him not to but didn't have the words. "Are you all right, my lady?" His voice was strained.

Uncertain, she gave a tentative nod. It was something, having him so close. The room was black as coal, but the smell of him made her eyes close so she could inhale.

His lips found hers and held for a moment as he eased himself between her legs—but not inside her. He skimmed his hand down her body. "You feel…good."

Oh, and so did he. The warmth of his closeness. The intimacy between them as they shared the same bed. She needed him to come closer.

"Thank you, my lord."

Thank you, my lord? What were they, in a drawing room discussing the rain over tea?

Manners and rules and proper ways of behaving had been drilled into her as far back as she could remember. How to walk, how to dance, how to converse. How to sit, how to pour, how to smile prettily and let a man talk so he wouldn't be threatened by any hint of female intelligence.

But there had been no schooling for *this* scenario. They were together. In bed. Nude. Skin against skin. Or at least, nude enough for what they were about.

Lord Bennington held himself above her. His…well, *he* brushed against her inner thigh. Then he settled against her most intimate place. And pushed. After an initial resistance, her body gave for him. He sank inside her.

He was big. Far bigger than anticipated.

Except instead of being frightening or uncomfortable, it was…well, it was quite wonderful, actually, the way he filled her. The way his body tensed as he slid deeper and deeper still, easing himself back and forth, back and forth, until he was fully planted.

He moaned. "You feel—oh, dear lord, my sweet wife, you'll be my undoing." He pushed up on his arms to place a kiss on her neck, his breath hot on her skin. "You're still all right, aren't you?"

"Yes."

"I can stop any time you want."

"No. Don't stop." It was as close as she could come to

admitting that, quite surprisingly, she liked this with him.

He moved with such tender gentleness, made all the more endearing by the way his body trembled as if shaken by the force required to hold back.

Then he thrust deeper—deeper than she would have ever imagined possible—and his body went rigid. Suddenly he was pulsing inside her.

With that, he collapsed atop her.

• • •

Jeremy, deeply seated inside his wife, panted for breath. It was the first time he'd ever been inside a woman without a barrier between his skin and hers. And it was a thousand times better than he could have ever imagined. Eliza was soft and wet, warm and snug…he shook with the effort of keeping himself in control. Of all the hellish improbabilities to come to pass, this had to be by far the sweetest.

Yes, he desired her. Yes, he well knew he was a man of unusual appetites. Yes, women were his most heinous vice. But of all the many couplings he'd given in to when he was weak and could no longer withstand temptation, none could compare with what he'd just had with her.

And yet, relations had never been so bloody awkward. He'd called their intimate relations "proceedings," for heaven's sake. Aloud. To her. What an ass he was. Were he one to rank his interludes objectively—and he wasn't—this one would fall near last. This was far closer to "exercising his conjugals," as he'd overheard a stuffy old viscount term it once, than he'd ever wanted to come.

But it had done one unexpected thing. It had lit a fire in him. All those other times… Well, they didn't matter, did they? And this one had.

With no small measure of regret at the loss of her body,

he slid out of her.

He was eager to have another go. Hard, too. Surely that would frighten her. With her he would *not* lose control. Could not. He liked her too much. And he wanted her to like him. Maybe even more, though it was difficult to say in the relaxed haze after intimacy. He wanted to couple with her again.

It wasn't enough for her to allow him into her bed. He needed her to want him in her bed. Which meant…hell, it meant he was going to have to seduce his own wife.

Wasn't a half-unpleasant prospect, that.

Unsure of what to make of these confused thoughts, Jeremy found his banyan on the floor and slipped back into his room.

He'd forgotten about the dog, though, and had to act on fast footing to avoid the tiny beast tearing out the moment he opened the door. The dog yapped once, as if to chide him, then went silent, presumably curling up in a warm spot against his mistress.

Jeremy closed the door with the lingering sensation that he hadn't done things quite as well as he ought. It was her first time after that good-for-nothing rotten bastard had tricked her into allowing him to…

A burst of rage pushed his heartbeat hard and fast. Lord help that lowlife Sir Domnall. It was all Jeremy could do not to leave immediately to hunt the bastard down and demand blood. He'd never known the thirst for vengeance like now, after learning what had happened to Eliza. How wretched it was to be powerless to avenge his wife for the pain and hurt inflicted upon her when she had been but a vulnerable innocent, desperate for love.

His thoughts gleefully murderous, he slipped into his own bed—cold and alone—with no small sting of jealousy. Of the dog.

Jeremy tried to settle back. He turned his head one way

then the other, trying to release the tension. After being with a woman, he was supposed to be relaxed. Sated. Instead, there was a knot in his stomach.

She'd been naught more than a child when that lowest of the low blackguard had exploited her. And what had he—Jeremy—done? He hadn't shown her that relations could be much better. It hadn't been his finest attempt. With Eliza it seemed like so much more was at stake.

If this had been a test, he wouldn't want to see his marks.

Pushing back the covers, he righted himself and drew a deep breath. That dratted door stood between them. *Again.* It was a theme with them. One he wanted to smash. All he had to do was open it. Seemingly so simple. In truth, there remained far greater barriers between them.

Sod it. If he was going to change things between himself and his wife, there was no time like the present. And he had to do a damned sight better than what he'd displayed, or she'd never want him in her bed again.

He still needed to break through her defenses. It didn't follow that he could do so by way of getting under her skirts. But it seemed as good a place to begin as any.

For the second time that night, Jeremy knocked on his wife's door. He waited until he was bidden to turn the knob.

By the light of a single candle, her face shone out of the darkness, pale and beautiful. Her eyes were huge, her cheeks pink. She was sitting up in bed, in the middle of all those rumpled covers, her hair down at last, one side of her shift fallen to expose a smooth shoulder.

The intimate sight settled the enormity of his responsibility on his shoulders. This woman was his *wife*. She deserved the best of everything. Including what they did together in bed. And he'd sooner see himself in hell than fail her.

"I came to apologize."

"Apologize?" She looked at him as if he'd gone mad.

"I didn't..." Dash it all. *Must this be so awkward?* All he wanted to do was give her the bedding she deserved. To show her what it could be like between a man and a woman. "I want another chance. If you'll allow me."

"Another chance..." She shook her head. The dog yipped. Eliza pulled the creature close and scratched his ears. "What are you talking about?"

"I mean between us. I'd like another chance to come into your bed."

"You may have all the chances you please, my lord."

"I meant tonight."

There was a pause. "So did I."

For the second time that night, Jeremy plucked the dog off the bed and banished her to the other room. This time, however, he had the sense not to speak. And when he slipped between the covers—wearing nothing but what he'd come into the world with—he didn't waste a single moment. Awkwardness could be damned. He wasn't going to allow that monster to reprise its ugly role between them. It had no place here. *He* was in charge. He had a duty to his wife to open her world to the pleasures of lovemaking. He would not fail her.

Her skin was nearly flawless. Smooth and even, with an occasional tiny dark-brown beauty spot like a constellation emerging in the dusk, star by star. By the light of the single candle, she veritably glowed.

Jeremy started at her neck. His mouth followed the curve, inhaling her uniquely feminine scent as he went, and smiling when she shivered. Her shift was still between them. He sat back and helped her to sitting, tugging the material from down about her legs, up and over her head, then turned his attentions to the small breasts pouting for his attention.

"What do you think, my lady?" He stroked a circle around a pale areola. "Shall I lick them? Suck them? Bite them?"

"I—I hardly know."

"Guess. If we guess wrong, then we'll have to try something else. Simple as that. Between us when we're here together, there will be no mistakes. I will never do anything you don't wish to have done." He forced himself to focus on what needed to be said. "You must promise me one thing. If you are ever uncomfortable, you will ask me to stop. I will always honor your needs—that is my promise to you."

She gave a nod. "I can agree to that."

"So which will it be, my lady?"

"Why don't you…do what you will and I'll tell you whether or not I find it…good."

"Good isn't enough. It must be *pleasurable*."

Her color heightened, and she dropped her gaze. "I don't know how I'll make that distinction."

"If you don't, banish me from your bed forever, my lady, for I won't be doing right by you."

He'd made vows before. Vows to himself. To his family. To his lineage. But never had he been more serious about anything in his life.

They tumbled back on the bed together. For the second time that night, he didn't reach for a sheath before thrusting himself between a woman's legs. It felt odd not to do so, but the wet heat of their skin-to-skin contact felt so very right. His teeth clenched together. It was taking all his strength to hold himself back.

More than anything, he needed to feel her come all over his cock. But he was too far gone. Helpless under the command of all his pent-up desire to do anything but continue as he was—moving, thrusting, touching her, kissing her.

It came too soon. His bollocks pulled up against his body, his abdominals tightened. And an excruciatingly powerful release dominated him. He pushed himself as far into her as her body would allow…

…and let everything go.

Chapter Twenty-Six

Eliza lurched into semiconsciousness, still knotted in the ropy vestiges of a nightmare. She was back at her mother's house, in her old room, and she'd avoided Domnall at a ball… but then had seen him at Corbeau's musical gathering…and smelled cherries…and…

And…

Oh, no.

She moved and came against an unexpected hard lump in her bed. A warm hard lump. A *nude* warm hard lump.

She blinked her eyes open. Beside her, Lord Bennington stirred just enough to take her into his arms and pull her close, her head settling in an unimaginably perfect place in the cradle of his shoulder. His body was hard and delineated with heavy musculature.

Her eyes fell shut again as she inhaled the scent of his skin. A bit of soap. A bit of musk. And with it, the memory of their…marital intimacies. They'd been together in Eliza's old bed. *In her mother's house.* Her cheeks singed with scorching heat. The way he'd felt against her…the way he'd tried so hard to be restrained…the hardness of him so deep and full within her. The way he'd left and returned again, determined to do better. To see her pleasured. It had all been infinitely better than expected.

And her husband's large hands were beginning to roam her body as if he wouldn't mind doing so again.

"Good morning, Eliza."

Daisy had come up from the end of the bed and was now trying to wedge herself between them. When that failed, the dog happily settled in the crevice between them both.

"Good morning, my lord." Eliza idly stroked Daisy's ears.

His hand found her backside and squeezed. "You're so lovely and generous there. It's quite a delight."

"My lord!" Cheeks hot, she squirmed out of his embrace and sat up. Daisy yipped at the sudden upset in her arrangement.

Eliza found him staring at her, wearing a devilish grin and nothing else. A wicked heat burned from the depths of his bejeweled eyes. "You can't mind so terribly if I admire your body, can you?"

A slant of lemony-yellow morning sun cut across the bed.

"I never thought about it."

"That I don't believe for an instant. Those deliciously low-cut bodices on evening gowns can't be for any other reason than to allow men to enjoy the view."

"Enjoy the view, indeed." She *tsked*. "The door is unlocked. You should go back to your own room before you're caught."

"It's early yet. I doubt very much there is any danger of that." His grin widened as he sat up. "I have a few other ideas on enjoying the view I'd like to explore. I'm a very hungry man before breakfast, you know."

The double meaning of his words was not lost on her.

He kissed her, hands settling upon her arms. "Do you want to try something? I think you'll like it."

Yes. "I—I suppose."

"Can I touch you?"

"You are touching me."

"No, can I *touch* you…everywhere. Would you like that?"

"Oh." A rush of heat to the place he no doubt meant told her that yes, yes, she would very much like to have him touch her there. She gave a careful nod.

But instead of touching her, he pushed from the bed. The sheets were rumpled with a ghostly imprint of his body.

Her mouth dropped open at the sight of him. The grace of his defined form as he plucked Daisy from the bed, sauntered across the room, put the dog next door, and came back again. Naked. And in quite the state of arousal.

He smiled when he caught her staring. "Like that bit, do you?"

Her cheeks burned. "Don't tease, my lord."

"I'm sorry." Back in the bed, he pulled her close. "It's all right if you do, you know."

"If I do what?"

"Like it. There's no shame in that." His voice was smooth and velvety rich. "You're a woman. It's perfectly natural to want to enjoy yourself with a man."

"Oh, stop talking and touch me." Before she went mad from the want of it.

"Happy to oblige." He eased her down and stroked his hand down her body before sliding it between her thighs.

What he was doing to her was something she could never have imagined possible. He stroked her gently—if she didn't know better, she might have said he was teasing her.

He rested beside her, running his lips over her cheek. "You've gone wet."

"I know."

"Do you want to be in charge?"

He was still running his fingers up and down, up and

down, pausing every now and again to give a nudge against that point at the top where all the best of everything was centered.

"I don't know what that means."

"You can do what you want…with yourself or with me."

"What would I do?" When Eliza tried imagining herself doing anything in this scenario, she came up short.

"Touch me. Touch yourself. You don't have to tell me what you want, you can show me. This, for instance…sit up."

"What?" But she was already doing as he'd commanded.

He remained splayed on the bed, his head flat against the mattress, the feather pillows bunched up and useless against the headboard. "If you've ever thought about trying to ride astride, now's your chance to practice."

"You can't possibly mean…"

The wicked grin returned. "Aren't you the least bit curious?"

With awkward trepidation, she balanced her weight on her hands while swinging a leg over his body. Her sex pulsed with mad longing, and the scent of arousal whispered a fragrant note in the air.

"I don't know if I can do this." She flicked her hair over her shoulders as she held herself stiffly above him.

But he began moving below her, rubbing the hard length of himself against the part of her that would take his body into her own. He sank his fingers into her thighs and gazed up at her. "You're so beautiful, Eliza. Sit down. Let me feel the weight of you on me."

She sat.

"Good. Now move your hips. Rub yourself on me. And when you're ready, you can take me and put me inside of you."

"Do…what?" She froze. He couldn't possibly mean…

"Take ahold of me and put me inside of you. When you're ready." He stilled, taking deep breaths. His hair was askew, his eyes glistening. "Unless this is too much too fast. If you're not enjoying it—"

"I don't know..." It wasn't quite the place to stop for a conversation. Her legs wantonly open and strewn over a nude male. Her hair down, her body bare, all of her fully exposed. It was a lot. To ask more...

"I'm going to have to do better than that, aren't I?" He reached down to take ahold of himself, positioning the tip at the proper place. "Here. I'll do it this time. That is...if you're ready."

Biting her lip, she gave a slow nod.

"Good. Now sit on me. Go gently—at your own pace."

She allowed her weight to sink down, his eyes fixed on the place he entered her. He might have been the one impaling her—slowly, deliciously filling her—but *she* was the one in charge. It was empowering and arousing, waking her body to a warm realization of the potential for sensual gratification.

"Move when you're ready, my lady." Jeremy laced his fingers into hers and squeezed, keeping ahold of her to brace her upright. "Close your eyes and let yourself do what feels good."

Eliza needed no further encouragement. She let her eyes fall shut and began moving her hips, rubbing herself against him where the nicest of the sensations originated.

Strange things were happening. Strange, wonderful things.

She kept moving, focusing entirely on the pleasure of the place where their bodies joined. Of them moving together. Of the feel of him against her and the delicious intimacy of the wanton position she'd taken above him.

She kept going and going until, quite unexpectedly, she dissolved into pure starlight.

Chapter Twenty-Seven

Eliza was in the carriage with Hetty and Fredericka. She and Hetty had taken the younger girl shopping on Bond Street.

Hetty made a pinched face and looked down her nose to affect her impression of the perfumist they'd encountered and punctuated her words with a sniff. "Very *ill-be-haved* young ladies, *in-deed*!"

The three of them burst into peals of laughter. Daisy, standing on Eliza's lap, joined in with an excited yip.

"I daresay, anybody who received that man's approbation is not somebody I wish to know." Fredericka giggled again.

"He's not the only perfumer in London." Hetty was shaking her head at the memory. "If he doesn't care for our custom, he shan't have it."

Fredericka nodded. "I think all the fragrances went to his mind and stripped away any sense of humor he might have had."

The carriage came to a stop before Lady Rushworth's house. Eliza had a sudden inspiration. "Why don't you two stay the next week with me?"

Hetty's round face flushed a rosy shade. "I'd love that. What about you, Fredericka?"

"I daresay my mother wouldn't notice if I didn't return home for a week."

"All the same, let's send her a note and ask her, and she can have clothing and things sent for you." Hetty might have enjoyed absurdities, but she had a remarkably logical head.

"I suppose, if we must."

One at a time, they climbed out, balancing a few of the boxes and parcels with them. Most of the stores would send items to their respective homes, of course, but there were certain purchases they'd wanted immediately. A pair of footman appeared to help them.

In the house, Caruthers rushed to Eliza. "Your mother wants you immediately."

She kept her expression placid for her friends. "Very well. I'll go up directly." She handed the dog over to Hetty's care. "Take Fredericka and Daisy up to the second drawing room and write that note, won't you?"

Stroking Daisy's ears, Hetty stepped close. "Are you sure we wouldn't be intruding on your mother?"

"She doesn't leave the first drawing room anymore."

"Really?" Taking off her bonnet and handing it to the servant with a smile of gratitude, she turned to Eliza. "I heard she was unwell, but…"

"I know." It didn't need to be said. Her mother's ailment was assumed to be more imagined than anything else. "I think my marriage affected her rather more strongly than anyone could have guessed."

The admission brought a twinge of guilt.

A few minutes later, though, going into her mother's room, the guilt evaporated. There was absolutely no part of her that wanted to fall in tears at her mother's feet and beg forgiveness. There was, however, a large part of her that wanted to flee back to Idlewood and forget she'd ever been a Burke.

But she was her mother's daughter, and here she needed to remain.

Lady Rushworth was in her usual place on the chaise longue, covered in rugs. Though it was a lovely day, a fire burned at the hearth. "What did I tell you about the Landon blood?"

"If you have something to tell me, Mother, pray speak plainly."

"They're not like us. They're interested in only what will help themselves. Take that *friend* of yours, Grace, for example—"

"Either you have something to say or you don't." Eliza was in no mood for her mother's thoughts about Grace.

"Your husband has ruined me."

"Mother, I don't mean any disrespect, but I very much doubt that."

Lady Rushworth slipped a folded sheet of paper from the wrinkles of the blankets and handed it to Eliza. "See for yourself."

Eliza skimmed the letter. "All this talks about is an investment gone bad."

Then her eyes caught on the amount, and the air went out of her lungs. "Mother, this number…it can't be right. If it were, it would mean you're—"

"Ruined. Yes. It's as I said. Unfortunately, it is right. I've already written to him about it and received a response."

Eliza's mouth went dry. "It's all you have. What are you going to do?"

"What can I do?" Idly, she fingered the gem-encrusted rings on her fingers. "That was everything I had. I'm destitute."

"You have your dower's portion, surely."

"It wasn't enough a hundred years ago, and it hasn't

changed a tuppence since then. But the worst part of this is that I have your husband to thank."

"What does he have to do with any of this?"

"It's his man of business who convinced mine that the venture was too big to fail. And look, now"—she punctuated her statement by stabbing a key clause in the letter with one finger—"it has. And I have nothing."

"I don't believe it." Eliza thrust the paper back to her mother and stuck out her chin. "I don't believe it, not for one minute."

"Trying to convince me or yourself, child?"

"Neither." She stood and paced to the other end of the room. "The earl wouldn't do such a thing. It's as simple as that. He might have been overeager in the business of eradicating his debt and he can be very single-minded, but he's not vindictive. If you lost money, he lost money, too. I don't think any man would go so far for such petty reasons." Eliza went to the mantel to fiddle with the china figurines displayed there.

"Were it to strip me of no more than a few thousand, I might agree with you. But to ruin me altogether—no, I think he *would* go that far. That's what Landons do. There are no half measures with them."

"It's not his fault. It's the fault of your man of business for making a phenomenally stupid mistake. Surely there has to be some sort of rule, written or otherwise, that says you don't put *all* your funds into a single venture." She dared a look back at her mother.

Lady Rushworth shrugged. "Think what you want. You always do." She sighed. "So headstrong. Just like your father."

If only her father were still alive. Things would have been so different. Lord Bennington would have seen Lord Rushworth about the debt, and her father would have graciously allowed him to repay it. Her mother never would have attempted to force Christiana's hand. Eliza never would have had to deceive the earl into marrying her.

At that last thought, a little hook caught in her heart. Would it be possible for something good to come out of all this?

She sank her teeth into her lip. Was it even fair to hope that something good might come out of what had started by such scandalous means? If any of this, any of it at all, started circulating among Society, it would follow them forever. That was the last thing her husband wanted. He'd done so much—given up so much—to rebuild after his uncle's spectacular scandal.

"What would you have us do, Mother?"

"The first thing that has to be done, obviously, is that he must leave this house at once. The second thing is to see the archbishop. It's time we started petitioning for this sham of a marriage to be annulled, once and for all."

Chapter Twenty-Eight

Jeremy hadn't set both his feet over the threshold of Lady Rushworth's house when Eliza was practically upon him.

"Thank goodness you're here at last." She and two other women—Lady Hetty and that young Chapman girl who had sung the other afternoon—were being put to rights by housemaids while the butler was organizing footmen about piles of trunks. He recognized his own among them.

"What's going on?"

"We're leaving." Eliza plucked Daisy off the floor to get him out from underfoot. "All of us. I've taken the liberty of sending a few servants over to open the Bennington house in Haight Square—we're going there."

"Immediately?"

"Immediately."

At her decided answer, he brought her into the seldom-used morning room at the back of the ground floor. "Let's discuss this over something that will settle our nerves."

"I thank you, but if you're talking about anything stronger than wine, I don't ever touch that, my lord."

He shut the door behind them.

The room overlooked the little garden. It was the space he'd made his own during his stay under Lady Rushworth's roof. He'd also stored a decanter of brandy on one of the side tables, replacing a hideous vase.

"I know you said you didn't want any"—he poured the golden-brown liquid into a glass and offered it to her—"but I suggest you reconsider your stance now. The fragrance alone is sometimes all it takes to bolster me."

She took his suggestion, inhaling the brandy but not sipping. Her lips were pale, her cheeks ashen.

They were silent for a long spell. Jeremy, with brandy of his own, took the seat opposite and waited. Silence could be painful—desperation beat in his chest to *do* something—but what he wanted and what Eliza needed were two entirely different matters.

"What's happened?"

It was the wrong time for such a question. Whatever it was, she wasn't ready to tell him. Jeremy sipped from his glass. The flavor burst on his tongue, hot at first, then settling back to oak and spiced fruit. It finished with a lingering hint of vanilla. "If you don't tell me, how can I help?"

"I've invited Hetty and Fredericka to stay with us. We'll be too crowded here, what with my mother always in the first drawing room." Daisy yipped for attention, and Eliza obliged, setting her brandy aside untouched, and placing a kiss on the dog's head.

"I see." There was something else, he was certain of it. But he wouldn't push her on the subject quite yet. "That will make it easier on my mother."

Eliza looked up at him, eyes wide in alarm. "Your mother?"

"She wants to pay a call on you. Don't worry, she's harmless." Truth be told, his mother was probably more desperate for Eliza to like her than the other way around. "You'll get on very well, I promise you. Wait and see."

The house Jeremy had taken at Haight Square for the new Bennington residence in London—the old one had been sold off to pay the former earl's debts after his death—was on the other side of Mayfair. The distance seemed unexpectedly serendipitous. The farther away from Lady Rushworth they were, the better.

Servants were busy with the tasks of opening the house when he arrived. They were Lady Rushworth's servants, not his own, and they worked as a favor to Eliza. They bustled about busily as if they'd been in service there for their entire lives. It took quite a while to make the house ready, so they were focusing on the necessities. The bedchambers, the kitchen, the dining room, and one sitting room. The rest—the more formal or less frequently used parts of the house—could be attended to later.

With Hetty and the young Miss Chapman in tow, Jeremy had to wait until a strategic moment when he could finally pull his wife aside. He took her into the library, Daisy at her heels. He took the protective cloth off the furniture in too hasty a movement, bringing up a huge cloud of dust.

They both coughed. "I apologize for that, my lady."

Daisy sneezed, then returned to the business of examining the room with his nose. Jeremy went to pour himself and his wife a drink. It would be his second in an afternoon, but he indulged so rarely, it hardly mattered.

Dabbing at her eyes with a handkerchief, Eliza shook her head when he offered her a glass.

"Can you tell me what's really going on now?"

"My mother is ruined."

Jeremy put the brandy back in a quick swallow, taking a moment to savor the burn. A stone had lodged itself in his stomach. What a misstep he'd made. There were so many places he could have prevented this—beginning by providing more oversight. This never should have happened. "And she blames me."

Which was only right. It *was* his fault. And he hated himself all the more because his carelessness could easily have ruined him. Then he'd be no better than his late uncle.

Eliza froze and slowly turned to him, expression cold. "You know about the investment, then?"

"I do."

"It's why your man of business called you to London, isn't it? That's your urgent business."

He wanted to deny it. He wanted to say he'd come because he hadn't been able to bear being parted from her. And when he'd seen her after their short separation, that was exactly how he'd felt.

But it wouldn't be the truth. "Yes."

"What are you going to do?"

"What can I do?" He leaned his head down in his hands and withdrew a long breath. "I thought at first I might cover the funds with my own. But I lost so much—I won't have anything near what I need to cover the amount until your dowry is fully transferred to me, and obviously it's too late for that now, at least without you or your mother being the wiser."

Her mouth fell open. "You weren't going to tell me?"

"I'm your husband."

"And that entitles you to what, precisely?" Her eyes sparkled with outrage, and her voice emerged low and tight. "I don't believe for a minute you have any right to decide to withhold anything from me. Pay me the compliment of respecting my ability to manage myself."

He ran his fingers through his hair. Insisting on anything with her, even so seemingly trivial a matter, made him no better than Lady Rushworth. "I know you can, my lady."

"Then why not tell me about the failed investments? That you ruined my mother?"

"It wasn't me, per se. But I do accept all responsibility. I should have been more vigilant about overseeing my affairs." A mistake he'd not make again.

"That didn't answer my question, my lord."

"I'm trying to protect you."

"Protect me?" She gave him an incredulous look.

"Yes. Why can't you see that?"

"Protect me from what, pray tell?"

From everything that might hurt her. She'd been under Lady Rushworth's twisted thumb for far too long. And he couldn't shake the haunting image of the innocent girl she'd been, hungry for love and attention, when she'd fallen into Sir Domnall's trap. The one thing he wanted to do above all was go back and prevent her from ever meeting the man. Not because he gave a hang about the state of her virginity. Hypocrisy aside, virginity was one of the stupidest things with which a man could be concerned. No. It was because he wanted to save her the pain.

"My lord, I understand that having control over your affairs gives you comfort. You like things a certain way, and I don't blame you. But you need to understand one thing. I'm not yours to manage, control, or protect. I'm too intelligent for that. So stop trying."

"This is not about your intelligence or your ability. I esteem both highly."

"Good. Then do me the honor of abiding by my wishes."

If he insisted further, she'd push him away. Maybe forever.

"I don't know if I can do that."

It was worse when his wife's features assumed that placid

expression she wore around her mother.

Her mask. A false impression of tranquility. Of submission.

He hated that look. And he hated himself more for provoking it.

"You must." As if to give him a glimpse into his fears, she rose. His heart started to pound, and panic squeezed the breath out of his lungs. If he lost her, what would he do? He wanted to reach out and take ahold of her. To pull her into his arms and never let her go.

But that was just it, wasn't it? He was holding on too tightly and doing everything wrong. So instead of reaching for her, he did nothing. While she swept from the room without a backward glance.

Chapter Twenty-Nine

In the small hours of the following morning, Jeremy slipped out of bed, made himself minimally presentable, and went down to the library at the back of the house. It was early enough that the sun hadn't chased all the night's shadows away. He lit some candles.

There was a box atop his desk. One he hadn't put there. He drew back the lid. Inside was his violin case. He opened it. The instrument had been repaired—restrung, the bridge righted, the horsehair on the bow replaced. Below the case was a packet of music tied together with a pink ribbon.

He placed the instrument under his chin, hummed an A, tuned, and drew out the first few shaky notes.

Jeremy winced. It had been too long. There was no hope in reclaiming what he'd lost. He'd have to accept this was one more thing he'd lost in the ruthless years when he'd done nothing but rebuild Idlewood.

The door opened. Eliza stood on the threshold holding Daisy. She was still wrapped in her night things, her dark hair in a braid falling over her shoulder.

An unexpected attack of mortification made him try to put the things away quickly. He didn't want her seeing him in a situation in which he wasn't a complete master of everything he touched. Especially after yesterday's row.

But she smiled as if their argument was the farthest thing from her mind. "You found it."

"What?" He clicked the latches on the case closed and set the box aside.

"I had it sent from Idlewood, and I took it to a luthier to be repaired."

She'd done this for him? His throat went tight. Other people didn't do things for him. He did things for other people. That was how the world was supposed to work. So he'd believed. What Eliza had done for *him*…it was like she'd found a little piece of him he hadn't known was thirsty until she brought cool water to his lips.

Unsure what to do with the muddle of emotion flooding his senses, he began pretending to shuffle and reorganize the papers atop the desk.

She came up beside him and put her hand on his back. He was wearing too many layers to feel warmth from her touch, but he would have sworn he did. She spoke gently. "It's not too late, my lord. If you want to bring music back into your life, all you have to do is begin to practice again."

"And make all the servants quit for the racket I'd make? I daresay not." He was trying to deflect her comment with humor. She didn't smile.

It was too close to other things in their shared life. If he could start fresh with music, maybe they could start fresh between them. He'd sworn never to forgive her. Now he cursed himself for ever having uttered such nonsense. Who was that man who'd spoken such harsh and unforgiving words? Not a man who could be worthy of Eliza.

A servant appeared with a message. Jeremy took it. Eliza

slipped away.

The note was from Isabel. "*The only thing I discovered about D. G. was that he isn't welcome at The Cloister.*"

The Cloister—nicknamed The Oyster for obvious reasons—was an exclusive brothel catering to exotic sexual requirements. The fearsome Bavarian woman who ran the place was as equally famous for what she would provide for her patrons as for what she wouldn't. While other places would do anything for money, The Cloister had *rules*. No girls or boys under sixteen. Nothing without the consent and approval of all participants. No animals. And absolutely no exceptions. They charged a good deal more than any other place in London, too. By all accounts, for good reason.

What Isabel had unearthed left too many unanswered questions—while at the same time turning Jeremy's stomach with the possibilities.

He rose and touched the edge of the paper to the candle, watching the paper blacken and curl as the flame consumed its prey. When he could hold it no longer, he tossed the last corner into the empty fireplace.

There was something happening to him. To *them*. Something that was enormous and frightening. He should have been afraid. He should have stayed away. Should have remained at Idlewood.

But he wasn't afraid, and he didn't want to stay away. He wanted to reach out and hold on with all his might and never let go.

An hour and some later, having made some hasty arrangements, he found himself in Eliza's room, where she was writing a letter before breakfast.

"We should take a little excursion today. We'd do well to take advantage of the fine weather. I've borrowed a barouche from an old school friend so we can go for a drive. Just you and me. We'll leave our troubles behind. What say you?"

"Borrowed a barouche?" She didn't look up, and her pen continued scratching its trail of curving black over the creamy sheet.

"The carriage is being repaired." The barouche was unfortunate. He'd wanted a carriage, and that's what he'd asked for. The friend in question—little more than an acquaintance, really—believing himself to be doing Jeremy a favor, had said he was sending the barouche instead. The better to enjoy the sunshine, he'd written in his note.

What Jeremy had wanted to enjoy was his *wife*. But a barouche was not the place for seduction.

She set down her pen and contemplated him a moment. "What about Hetty and Fredericka?"

Damn. He'd forgotten about their guests.

"Ah. Yes. You and me and your friends." Jeremy hoped he didn't sound too enthusiastic or else she would know immediately how insincere he was being. "Of course. We can't leave them behind."

So they all went. All four of them, with Daisy making the fifth of their party.

Eliza arranged her skirts, keeping her movements slight and ladylike, as if by doing so she could make herself smaller. It wasn't as if she were consciously trying to be invisible. Instead, it was as if she'd done it for so long, she now did it without thinking. Was he imagining things, or had she always done that? Searching his memory, he handed Daisy to her.

The day was bright. The sunshine soaking London made the habitually gray days seem like an invention of a bad dream.

Hetty settled into the bench next to the girl, leaving Jeremy and Eliza the seat opposite to themselves. "Where are we going, my lord?"

"Have any of you ladies ever visited Kew Gardens?"

They shook their heads.

"Good." As he spoke, the only one who appeared visibly pleased to be out was Daisy, the dog appearing to grin as his tongue hung from his mouth. "Then we shall all see them together."

Kew Gardens meant going all the way to Richmond. No insignificant distance.

It was worth it when they arrived and Eliza smiled. "It's lovely."

Jeremy looked up at her as he helped her down from the conveyance. "I couldn't agree more."

Seeming to understand him perfectly, her gaze fell, and her cheeks filled with color.

When she took his arm, he swelled with pride. The most beautiful woman in the world was on his arm—was his wife—and everyone could see.

They left the driver with the carriage and wandered into the park. There were few other people around. When Fredericka ran ahead, the dog dashed after her. With a whoop of delight, Hetty followed in the chase, leaving Jeremy and Eliza quite alone.

The lush gardens were the embodiment of English beauty. Green, picturesque, and neither too tamed nor too wild.

Would Eliza be shocked if he tried to slip away to a remote corner and share an intimacy or two? Jeremy couldn't help but grin. Perhaps it was time to begin pushing the boundaries to see how he could delight her further.

And if they were caught? The risk made it all the more exciting. It would be scandalous—the last thing Jeremy had thought he could ever want. But to be discovered with his wife in his arms? Well, that didn't seem *so* bad.

It didn't entirely make sense, he had to admit. Then again, people were full of idiosyncrasies. Why should he be any different? The fact of the matter was, he liked intercourse. And he liked it with his wife—though he had yet to show her the act could be all he knew it could be.

"There's so much to see here. Where shall we begin, my lord?"

"How about there?" He pointed to a copse of trees along the periphery. Between her closeness and his lascivious thoughts, he was half hard.

She hesitated, as if trying to puzzle out what he could want in a place so far away. "That's away from everything else, I believe."

"Let's wander through."

"Very well."

Under the shade of the towering trees, she stopped and drew away to turn and admire the quiet spot. "It's quite lovely here, actually."

He came to stand before her. She was of an average height and build, but he felt so large and clumsy next to her. Her natural grace was evident in every line of her features and her every movement.

Awareness bloomed in him. Awareness of himself as a man. Of her as a woman—a desirable woman. And of how the world had shrunk so that only they two existed.

"I've missed you, you know." He reached for her, drawing her close. She smelled like roses, and it was driving him mad.

"I'm right here," she whispered. Eliza lowered her eyes, cheeks pink. The air between them became heavy with mutual recognition. The way her color heightened told him her thoughts were not far from his.

"I think you know what I mean." His voice came out gravelly. This was taking a turn toward seduction.

Perfect. It was an opportunity he wasn't about to miss.

• • •

Eliza was pinned between a tree and her husband. In that

strip of exposed flesh below the ribbons of her bonnet and above the neckline of her bodice, his lips traced over her skin. "This is wrong, my lord."

"What's wrong about it?"

"You *know* what's wrong about it."

"A husband and a wife doing precisely what it is that the married state allows them to do together without risk to their immortal souls?" The low depths of Lord Bennington's voice made her shiver with want. The smell of him drew her closer so that he might imprint himself upon her skin.

His lips grazed hers. She tilted her head to take his kiss, but he drew back a fraction. Just enough to tease her. "I want to do things to you, my lady. Things people hardly speak of."

"I think that's quite evident enough, my lord."

"You don't understand. First I want to kiss you and taste you between your legs. Then I want to wedge you between myself and the trunk of this tree and hike your skirts up to your waist and drive myself into you again and again and again. I want to make you cry out with pleasure so loudly, they hear you in London."

Eliza's face stung with heat. "I can't believe we're talking like this."

The earl smiled down at her. "But you like it, don't you?"

"Much more than I ever expected, my lord."

It didn't feel as wanton as it sounded. Not just any man would extract such a response from her. Quite the contrary. Other men left her cold. They always had, ever since she'd been ruined. Thank Providence she hadn't married Captain Pearson. She'd never have discovered this side to herself. And she *liked* this side to herself.

Lord Bennington smiled with what could only have been described as fierce masculine pride.

Then he kissed her. It wasn't like any kiss that had come before. It was deeper. Slower. It wasn't simply ordinary physical need that drew them together, but something much more profound. Much rarer.

The earl knelt.

"What are you doing, my lord?"

"I'd like to show you something, my lady. Something I've wanted to do for a long time." He looked up, hands on his skirts. "May I?"

"We're in the middle of a park."

"In a secluded area where nobody will find us."

He pushed the fabric up past her knees, past her stockings, all the way up to her waist. She was fully exposed. Or so she thought until he nudged her thighs open and leaned in to put his mouth—*oh!*

She would have objected had he not then moaned with undisguised pleasure.

Eliza's head fell back. That was his tongue. On her…*there.* It was warm and luxurious, soft and exhilarating.

"I want this." She didn't know where it had come from, but once it was past her lips, there was no regret. Only empowerment. It was what *she* wanted. This wasn't only for him. This wasn't because they were married and trying to create an heir. This was for *her.*

He glanced up at her. The wicked glee in his smile would have warmed the devil's own heart. "Tell me again."

She spoke with hard-earned certainty. "I want this."

"Make me."

"I'm sorry?"

"I want you to show me what you want, my lady. Make me pleasure you."

Not knowing what else to do and desperate to resume, she pushed his head back between her legs. "Don't stop."

And he didn't. She let everything else go. The entire world became about what he was doing to her with his mouth. Her hips rocked, her breath came fast and hard. She rode the sensations higher and higher, eager and greedy for what was coming.

She hit the climax, and pure pleasure shot through every limb.

When it was over, she collapsed against the tree, her legs nearly unable to support her weight. She caught her breath as the earl rearranged her clothing and came to his feet. He kissed her. "That was incredible. You're so beautiful. You were made for this, you know."

Made to come alive in his hands. Startled by the stray thought, she pulled upright. "What's happening?"

"I think you know quite well, my lady," he all but purred.

"I mean, what's happening between us?" Because she couldn't bear it if it came to naught.

She wanted to ask him if he'd forgiven her for her deception. The words stuck on her tongue like they'd been glued with bitter treacle. She wasn't prepared to hear his answer. Not when it very well might be no. She didn't need her heart involved in this debacle between her and the earl.

Except that was exactly what had happened, hadn't it? Along this treacherous road they were traveling together, her heart had softened. Was it when he'd given her Daisy? Or perhaps when she'd told him how she'd been ruined and he'd gone mad with rage against Sir Domnall. Perhaps when he'd unwittingly exposed his love for his mother. Or maybe it had been the look on his face when she'd told him she'd repaired his violin.

She could never have guessed he'd be such an easy man for whom to have strong feelings. He was hard and determined to the point of ruthlessness, willing to marry to pay a debt, all else be damned. His instinct to protect her from harm worked against him.

But these were small flaws in the face of everything else. They made him all the more precious. He was no saint…

and all the more deserving of love for the plain fact that he needed love.

He traced a line down the side of her face. "Where are you, my lady? You're here with me, but you're a hundred miles away."

She pulled herself close to him, resting her head on his chest and closing her eyes to enjoy the scent of wool and starch and clean male. "I'm right where I want to be."

Around them, the leaves on the trees rustled in a slight breeze. It was as if nothing could ever go wrong again.

Chapter Thirty

The next afternoon, in the drawing room in the Haight Square house, Eliza's stomach dropped when Templeton came to announce that Sir Domnall and Lady Tutsby had come to collect Fredericka.

She rose, shaking. Hetty and Grace had taken the girl to pay a call on Grace's sister Isabel, so Eliza must face the two of them alone.

Slipping from the room, she almost collided with Lord Bennington. His face was grave. "I just heard. I'm coming with you."

She held up a hand. "I will handle this by myself, if you please."

"You can't see them alone."

Silently as a ghost, Templeton made a strategic exit.

"I can see them alone, my lord, and I will. I don't need your help."

"Don't need my help, or don't want my help?"

Eliza raised her chin at him. "Both. So it works out nicely, doesn't it?"

She swept from the room.

Lady Tutsby stood a little before Sir Domnall. With the merest glance at the man who'd caused her so much shame and anguish, Eliza's skin crawled. Once upon a time, she'd let that man *touch* her. And so much more. How could she have been so stupid?

She prayed she hid her disgust as she bade them welcome. "Won't you stay long enough for me to offer you both some refreshment?"

The feathers on Lady Tutsby's bonnet fluttered as she shook her head. "Thank you, my lady, but I've come to collect Fredericka. I have other matters to attend to this afternoon."

"Of course, my lady." Eliza tried to show deference where she felt none. Fredericka was safe—for now. "We thought you were coming tomorrow, however, and I'm afraid she's not here."

"I'll just stay to collect her things and see her home, then. I don't mind waiting."

Smiling as sweetly as could be, Eliza cut a look directly to Sir Domnall. She wagered that, in his quest to fool Lady Tutsby into believing he wanted to marry her, the man had made one significant omission. "And how is your wife, Sir Domnall? I do hope Lady Gow is well."

Beside him, Lady Tutsby blanched. Her lips formed a thin line as she turned to the man. "Your…*wife*?"

Good. She hadn't known.

To his credit, the knight didn't try to deny the existence of his spouse.

He shot Eliza a look of unadulterated hatred. She held her head high. She regretted nothing. The man was repugnant.

She'd bested him. She'd kept Fredericka away from his grasp. That was the most important thing.

Lady Tutsby covered her mouth, eyes wide with the hurt of betrayal, and she ran from the house. The door slammed behind her.

The potent sensation of sweet triumph made Eliza drunk with happiness. She could have whirled, just like Christiana had that day Tom had come to Idlewood to claim her for his bride.

But the mood was short-lived. Eliza and Sir Domnall were alone. The last time they were alone, he'd…

He stepped close, forcing her to step backward until she ran up against a wall. Wincing and trying to breathe from her mouth so she wouldn't smell him, she turned her head, not wanting to see the lines and pores of his skin. Not wanting him so close. Not wanting such stark evidence of just how powerless she remained.

Her mouth was dry, and her heart pounded.

His voice was hard, his face pinched in disapproval. "Quite the family you married into, the Landons. Guess it's true what they say about the Landon blood."

Eliza's fingers flexed. The man deserved to have his eyes clawed out. Eliza had been so angry that summer. Surely part of her blindness to the man's nature had been willful. She had half a mind to spit in the man's face. "I'd take the worst of them on their darkest day over *you* on your best."

His eyes narrowed to slits. "You've done a very foolish thing with Lady Tutsby, my girl. I have no compunction against exposing your shame. Wait until all of London is tittering about what you did. You'll never live it down."

Eliza pushed him away with a strength she hadn't known she possessed. She couldn't let him see how he frightened her or how she feared exposure. "Leave me alone."

Alone being the important word. Far better to keep the world ignorant. It was preferable to the isolation and ostracizing she'd experience if it became known what she'd done all those years ago. The repercussions of such a scandal would ruin the rest of her life. The news might actually kill her mother. And she'd lose Jeremy. He might think he wanted vengeance on her behalf now. If she mired him and his family in public humiliation, however…

Sir Domnall stumbled backward. His eyes narrowed, and he straightened his hat and tugged his jacket. "This isn't over, pet. You'll be sorry for this. Very sorry, indeed."

Chapter Thirty-One

Jeremy had only caught a glimpse of what transpired in the entrance hall, but what he'd seen would eat at his soul for an eternity.

Before he could do anything, the bastard stormed out the door and Eliza ran up the stairs in tears.

Jeremy was helpless against the force of his rage. It was unlike anything he'd ever experienced. Everything else he'd ever been angry about in the past had crumbled to insignificance in the face of seeing Eliza threatened.

A moment ago he'd been himself. What he'd seen had changed him, maybe forever. Shaking with the intensity of his thirst for blood, he stalked down the corridor and tumbled down the steps into the street. The world around him was an incoherent mixture of incomprehensible sounds and blurry images. Everything seemed too fast and too bright. Afternoon sunlight glared from all surfaces, everything still wet from a passing shower.

His sight homed in on the back of that monster of a man who'd hurt his wife. She'd claimed she'd been a willing participant, but no doubt the baseborn worm had used his wiles to get from her exactly what he'd wanted.

And then he'd heard that vile son of a dog tell her, *I have no compunction against exposing your shame. Wait until all of London is tittering about what you did. You'll never live it down.*

Jeremy saw visions of his family burning in infamy all over again. Not only Eliza, but his cousins, who were only just regaining tenuous footing in Society. After all they'd suffered, they couldn't endure more. Not if he could help it.

Before he knew what he was doing, Jeremy grabbed the revolting man by the shoulder and spun him around.

In the back of his mind, Jeremy was dimly aware of gasps from nearby onlookers. A coach on the road slowed, and two round faces appeared in the window, pointing and whispering.

Let them look. This was what they wanted, wasn't it? To see the next generation of Landons give them something to talk about well into the winter months? A perverse part of him wanted to give them exactly what they wanted, consequences be damned.

"What is the meaning of this?" Sir Domnall glared, brushing at his shoulder where Jeremy had grabbed him.

But there was no time for words. Jeremy's fist cracked against the man's jaw.

Sir Domnall sprawled backward, tumbling onto the ground. He touched his face tenderly, grimacing as if it ached. "What have you done, you stupid man?"

"Hyde Park." Jeremy spoke from between clenched teeth. "Tomorrow at dawn. Choose your second."

He turned on his heel, leaving the other man in the street as he returned to his wife. This wouldn't be over until that bastard was *dead.*

• • •

After her interaction with Sir Domnall, Eliza's nerves were a jumble. It was difficult to be certain, but her husband also seemed preoccupied.

After dinner, she approached him gently. He sat in a big chair by an empty fireplace with his nose buried in his newspapers. They were alone, Hetty having sent a note that the three of them were going to dine with Lord Bennington's mother and Isabel. "Something seems to be weighing on your mind."

He glanced at her over his reading material, returning a tight smile. "Nothing of the sort, I assure you."

She took the seat next to him. "You're not protecting me from anything again, are you?"

He took a beat too long to respond. "No."

Eliza's heart sank. He was lying. She paced to the other side of the room. She stared at the pictures on the wall a moment, not really seeing beyond the superficial in the landscapes captured so carefully in oils.

She turned and drew a breath. "Sometimes it seems like we're becoming closer. Other times, it feels as if we're still as much strangers as we were the day we married."

He folded the newspapers, tossed them aside, and stood. Every time he went from seated to standing, she was reminded of how large the man was. It seemed as though the surprise should have worn off by now. "I want to do something for you."

"My lord…" Her words evaporated to nothing when he left the room. When he returned a minute later, he carried his violin case.

"I can't guarantee I'll produce anything worth hearing."

Her heart fluttered as he began to rosin the bow. He tuned and positioned the instrument under his chin. She licked her lips.

He pulled the bow, and the music began. Eliza recognized

Telemann, though she couldn't have named the piece. It was wistful, but also graceful. Jeremy played extremely well, although not perfectly. With a touch of practice, he would be quite good. When the piece finished, he paused momentarily before moving to a Bach violin solo.

If he'd really not touched the violin for so many years, it was amazing that he could still recall the notes. Maybe they were gone from his mind but lived in his fingers, as it sometimes was with her and a poem she'd had to memorize in the schoolroom. She couldn't remember the words when she tried to speak them, but once she sat with a pen, it all came out. Hours upon hours of having to write out passages again and again had stayed with her.

Then he put the instrument down, shaking out his left hand and flexing his fingers as if the exercise had made them stiff.

"Can't you play a bit more? I do so love music."

"My fingertips can't take any more just now, I'm afraid." He snapped the latches on the case and then looked to her, deadly serious intensity shining from the fiery aquamarine depths of his eyes. "Do you trust me?"

Eliza shook her head, not understanding. His playing hadn't been merely playing, but what it had meant, she couldn't see. "I want to."

"But you don't?"

"Not really."

The earl looked away. "I'm going out for a bit."

"What?" She frowned. "At this hour?"

"I need to think."

"Which you can't do here?"

"It's too confining. I need to move." He placed a kiss on her forehead. "Don't wait up—I don't know when I'll be back."

Eliza only sputtered. She was speechless. He was actually

leaving?

Sure enough, he disappeared through the door. It took a moment for her brain to catch up with what had happened. She was alone—and in more ways than one. Alone. He'd left her *alone*. First he'd shut her out and then he'd abandoned her.

It would have been easy to crumble to the floor. Part of her wanted to. If she did, though, she might never be able to stand again—figuratively speaking. The part of her that wanted to be strong spurred her forward. She ran after Jeremy, dashing through the corridor.

But she was too late. The front door shut behind him. Templeton, who'd seen his lordship out, turned to catch sight of Eliza, his brows rising a little. "My lady? Is there something you require?"

Inwardly, Eliza squirmed. In her mother's home, the servants had been her collaborators. They'd been proud of their service to her father. After his passing, they'd stayed for her as much as to honor his memory. Here everything was different. She had to remember that while they were loyal, she was still new here, and there were certain ingrained hierarchies that were to be both observed and respected. "Please send Margaret up."

It was well past midnight when there came the sound of the doors to Eliza's bedchamber quietly opening. Daisy leaped up from her spot by Eliza's hip and started yipping at the newcomer, who stepped across the floor in hasty yet careful steps. He must have removed his boots. His footfalls were soft.

He was home. Her heart lifted in cautious hope.

"*Shh*, you silly dog. It's just me," Jeremy whispered. "Don't wake your mistress."

Eliza pushed herself up on her elbows and stared into the blackness. A sliver of light came through the crack in the door. She could see just enough of him. "I wasn't asleep."

He began peeling away his jacket. It fell to the floor. An item at a time, the rest of his clothing followed. Then he slipped under the covers and reached for her.

As he took her close, she shivered with warm anticipation and inhaled. She'd expected him to smell of alcohol or smoke. He smelled of neither. The scent of the clean outdoors clung to his skin, as if he'd been caught in a spot of rain.

Instead of initiating another round of heir making, he curled close to her and held her tight. They lay together in the dark, neither of them speaking. How long, she couldn't have said. She'd thought he'd gone to sleep when he moved and pressed a hard ridge against her hip.

"Do you want to, my lady?" He kissed her neck.

She nodded.

He pushed the covers down and took her night rail up, pulling it over her head and casting it aside. His hand skimmed the surface of her bare skin. She shivered with warm longing and erupted into gooseflesh. When his fingers dipped between her legs, she let out a shaking moan of longing. "I never knew it could be like this."

"I know." He continued touching her, stroking gently and building sensation slowly. "Are you ready?"

All she could do was nod again.

"Tell me you want me."

"I want you."

The earl positioned himself above her on his elbows, opening her legs and putting himself between them. Pressing the tip of his erection against her entrance, he began entering her.

Her breath caught, and she arched her back.

He froze. "Am I hurting you?"

Eliza shook her head. "You're large, is all. But it feels good…the way you…"

"Say it." His voice was raw. Needy. And when she braced her hands against the steel strength of his arms, she found him trembling. He was so tense. As if it took all his willpower to hold himself back.

She had so much power over him. The realization came with a heady rush of arousal, and she almost unexpectedly hit her climax then and there.

"The way you…" Heat burned her face. In the dark, he could not see the violence of her blush. It made her daring. "…fill me."

He slid the rest of the way in and hissed as if in pain.

"Oh…" Her fingers dug into his back. "My lord, I—"

"I think…" He was deep in her body. "I think it's time you called me Jeremy."

"Oh, my lord, I don't—"

"Say it, Eliza. I need to hear it. I need to hear you say my name."

"Jeremy."

Inside her, his cock flexed. He began to move. "Yes. Again."

"Jeremy."

"Oh, yes. My sweetest Eliza, you have no idea what you do to me." He reached between them and worked his fingers in circles on the site of her greatest pleasure as he continued to thrust into her.

They moved together. She was at once herself and part of something greater—something she could only have with him.

Chapter Thirty-Two

Last night when Jeremy made love to Eliza, he'd been so warm. She'd been soft, and her body had welcomed his so sweetly. But he hadn't told her that he had been saying goodbye to her.

When he'd imagined himself here about to face Sir Domnall, he'd thought he'd feel strong and righteous. Instead, he was nothing but cold and alone.

The morning was soggy. It had rained during the night, leaving droplets clinging to the grass and leaves. Mist covered the earth, muffling sound.

Jeremy sat on the carriage step, staring at his hands. Once he'd made music with them. Pressed the tip of each finger into a string while pulling a bow across the other end.

Now he was going to kill a man. Or do his damnedest to try.

And then what? Flee England? Leave Eliza forever?

He'd worked so hard to master his control. And had failed at the most critical moment. So many years rebuilding the Landon name after his notorious uncle's scandalous downfall, and this was where he'd ended up. Fighting a duel.

But every time he thought of how Sir Domnall had had Eliza pushed up against a wall, he thirsted for blood all over again.

"Don't worry." Corbeau, Jeremy's second, came from behind the carriage to clap him once on the back. "Nobody thinks you've done the wrong thing."

The words almost didn't suit the man. But Corbeau continued. "Had any man threatened my wife, I'd have done the same. Without the least hesitation."

If only Corbeau knew. It wasn't a mere bodily threat. Jeremy was willing to accept the scandal of the duel if it meant stopping the greater scandal of what Sir Domnall had done to his wife. It wasn't fair, but Society would scorn *her* for what had happened, and the Landons would suffer for it.

No small part of him hated each and every person in all of England for their righteous hypocrisy. He couldn't suffer those fools ever again. What a man was forgiven would ruin a woman forever. It was hateful, that set of contrasting principles. But that was the world they lived in. And if a duel meant protecting his family, a duel it would be.

Trying to keep in check the fiery ball of rage threatening to consume him, Jeremy squinted at a man with curly golden hair who had come with Corbeau. "I'm sorry. We've met but… who are you again?"

"Sir Harold Alcott."

"Ah. Yes. The ball. Forgive me, but what are you doing here? I could have sworn you didn't like me."

"I don't. And I'm not here for you. I'm here because I'm a friend of your wife."

A carriage approached, coming at some speed. Before it was fully stopped, Eliza was tumbling down and running toward him. The hem of her gray skirts darkened with the damp from the ground.

Jeremy stiffened. "You weren't supposed to know. How did you find out?"

"Margaret told me."

For a resentful moment, he wished he'd insisted Eliza find herself a new maid. But the feeling quickly deflated. Vengeful anger had brought him here this morning. If he was to die, he didn't want to leave this world with the burdens of resentment, anger, or regret on his soul.

But he did have regret. Regret that he'd put living aside and focused so hard on the estate. Regret that he hadn't forgiven Eliza sooner, forgotten what she'd done, and rejoiced in their being together. Life wasn't about one's reputation.

If only he'd never put down his violin. If only he'd set aside his absurd dislike of London sooner and attended the Season, if only in the name of making friends. If only he'd never turned his back on his cousins' lives.

The laments he didn't want to carry to his grave weren't making the situation any easier. "You shouldn't be here. This is no place for a lady."

She ignored him. And good on her. There was that power of spirit he'd first admired in those secret letters she'd sent him. "Don't do this, Jeremy, please. It's not worth it."

Corbeau sidled away and went to help the other coachman with the horses.

"I have to." Jeremy was aware of Sir Harold's lingering stare and of the sadness in his eyes before the man moved to follow Corbeau.

"Don't take this risk. I don't want to be widowed."

"I don't plan on leaving you a widow." His words were boosted with no small measure of bravado. He was all too aware of the stark reality of the situation. Death could be hovering behind him even as they spoke.

"Please. Call this off. I beg of you."

"I can't."

"Why? For honor's sake?"

Jeremy ran his fingers through his hair. His pulse beat steady and hard. "He hurt you."

"I've told you, it's none of your concern. What happened was years ago. Long before you."

"He deserves to *suffer*."

"It doesn't matter." She stepped back from him, dark eyes huge in her fair face. Her lips were parted. A wisp of hair played in an errant breeze. "Don't do this. Run him out of London if you want—nobody will be sorry to see the back of him, I'm certain. But don't fight this duel. I'm not a damsel in distress, he's not a dragon, and you are not St. George."

"What else am I supposed to do?"

"Forget honor. Forget Sir Domnall. Forget any of this."

"I can't."

Eliza tugged on Jeremy's arm. "What will become of me if you're dead?"

That stopped him cold.

A horse approached at a fast clip, the sound of the hoofbeats preceding the appearance of the rider. But instead of Sir Domnall, Arthur appeared from the mists. He saw Jeremy, and his mouth split into a grin. "I didn't believe it when I heard. My upstanding brother who can do no wrong"—he spoke mockingly—"would never participate in a duel. Think of the scandal."

Jeremy waited for the annoyance to rise, but it didn't come. There were too many other emotions taking precedence in his breast. He had no room, no time for anything else. Still, it wasn't precisely a happy reunion. "What are you doing here?"

His brother swung down from the horse. "I had to see for myself, of course."

"Of course."

"That and Mother would have my hide if I weren't here in case of injury or death to her favorite son." He gave a terse smile.

"If you think that, you're more a fool than I ever believed you to be." Jeremy grabbed Arthur by the arm and made his brother face him. "When this is over, things are going to be different. I don't know what happened to make us enemies, but that's not how I want things to be—not anymore. We're family. We must be loyal to one another."

The thoughts brought a powerful resurgence of determination pounding through Jeremy's veins—determination to finish Sir Domnall once and for all. To fight for Eliza so she didn't have to fight alone.

All his brother did was give a careless shrug and turn on his heel, walking away.

Another carriage approached. Jeremy tensed. When the conveyance stopped, Sir Domnall stepped down. The wind caught, blowing the longish ends of his sandy hair.

"I'm sorry I wasn't pure for you." Eliza's voice wavered. She spoke softly. For his ears only. Her eyes fell shut, and a heavy tear rolled down her cheek. "I'm sorry, please believe me, I'm so desperately sorry. But this won't change anything."

Not believing what he was hearing, Jeremy stared at his wife. "You don't really believe I think any less of you because you weren't a virgin, do you?"

"Of course you must."

Jeremy gave Sir Domnall a hard look. This was his fault. And she didn't want him to rip this rotten blackguard limb from godforsaken limb?

But before Jeremy could call the whole thing off, the other man cast Eliza a look of pure scorn and sneered. "I broke her in well, didn't I, my lord? I hope you enjoyed her as I did."

Eliza's fingers dug into Jeremy's arm as she struggled to keep him in her grip. "Don't give in to him. He's trying to bait you."

Sir Domnall stepped close, his eyes spitting daggers, and

spoke in a low voice. "All this trouble over a worthless *whore*. Tell me, Lady Eliza—pardon me, Lady Bennington now, isn't it? How many others have you spread your legs for as easily as you did for me?"

Jeremy's control turned to ash. That despicable apology his wife had given him—Sir Domnall was the one responsible for making her feel she was less worthy. The horrid man had all but outright forced her, and she was the one who apologized.

It wasn't right. The world would never be a better place until men like Sir Domnall could no longer hurt people in pursuit of their own godless pleasures.

Jeremy wrenched from his wife's grasp. His veins burned with blood heated to a steaming boil. "If you live to see the sunset tonight, Domnall Gow, you worthless, blue-deviled swine, it won't be because I didn't try."

Sir Domnall offered a mockingly flourished bow.

The pistols were checked. The paces called. Jeremy stood alone in the field staring into a bleak morning, the sound of his breathing unnaturally loud to his ear. The firearm was heavy and cold in his hand.

It was like he'd stepped from his own body and watched the proceedings from a distance. He was disassociated from everything.

Somehow, he knew to turn. His fingers squeezed. There was a click. A burst of smoke. A crack and a jolt. And then an acrid scent wiped away all trace of the air's wet morning sweetness.

Sound came as though he were submerged underwater. Shouting.

And a burst of pain.

Then…slowly, as if falling from a great height, he was swallowed into a black abyss.

Chapter Thirty-Three

Eliza wiped perspiration off her brow and dipped the rag into the porcelain basin. Red permeated the clear water, contrasting with the stark white of the vessel.

Blood. Jeremy's blood.

She sat on a stool next to the sofa where he'd insisted upon being placed after refusing his bed. "Only invalids take to their beds," he'd bitten out when they'd brought him home, jaw clenched in pain he refused to acknowledge.

They were alone in the upstairs drawing room, but the house was far from empty. Lord Corbeau and Sir Harold had returned with them, trying—without success—to be helpful. It wasn't that either was an incompetent man, but it was an unusual situation. Nobody quite knew what to do—except on one score. Lord Corbeau was a force in Parliament. Very few men risked being on his bad side. For that, he promised to see that the powers of the land overlooked the fact that Jeremy had so publicly flouted the law. Corbeau didn't make promises he didn't intend to keep, so Eliza was free from worry.

Jeremy's brother had come with them, too, though his

motivations were less clear. He didn't seem to want to help, although he appeared uncharacteristically gray faced and thin lipped. It hadn't taken long before Grace and Hetty had arrived—and thank heaven for them. Eliza had sent them a pleading look. They'd exchanged a glance and herded the men out of the room. The whole lot of them were now in the breakfast room.

The doctor had been and gone, leaving instructions to keep the wound clean and the patient fed, quiet, and dosed liberally with laudanum as required.

She brought the warm cloth to the injury. Jeremy hissed as she gently pressed it against him. The bullet had grazed him, tearing away a notch in his upper arm. Stitches, darkened to black and hardened by blood, stood in a neat line on the swollen area.

Sir Domnall hadn't been so lucky, taking a bullet in his thigh. They'd received word that it had missed the artery and hadn't shattered the bone. So long as his wound didn't fester, he'd live.

Eliza wasn't sure how she felt about that. She couldn't hope for death. Not even for him. It wasn't that he didn't deserve it, but such a desire would mar her soul. And that she couldn't permit. The man had cost her too much to allow him that, too. But would it be so terrible to wish he'd been incapacitated? Or horribly disfigured. That would have done, too.

Jeremy winced.

"If you're in pain—"

"No. No laudanum. I hate that stuff." He grimaced. "I won't be without my reason."

"Then what made you fight that duel?"

"What?"

She bent her head and spoke softly. "It wasn't for me."

"What are you talking about?" His brow furled. "Of

course it was for you. How could you think anything else?"

"Never mind." As much as she'd thought about needing to have this conversation with Jeremy, it was too soon. The pain was too acute. When she'd seen the rage take hold of him…seen him lift his weapon and point it at Sir Domnall…it had crushed her heart. "Now's not the time for this discussion. You're newly injured and—"

He stayed her hand and spoke between clenched teeth. "Now *is* the time. Tell me."

Eliza withdrew her hand from his grip and rinsed the cloth in the basin again. She didn't meet his eye and took a shaky breath. "You let your rage get the better of you."

"That vile b—pig *hurt* you."

"Yes." The water in the porcelain was turning dark. "And it wasn't your fight to fight."

"You're my wife."

"And that means *you* make decisions for me? Besides…" Her voice turned soft. Her next words took a certain amount of courage, because they opened a tender vulnerability that Jeremy might or might not accept. If he didn't, she didn't know how she would stand it. "What use would your heart have been if you'd gotten it shot through?"

A dark shadow crossed his face. "Who said anything about hearts?"

Eliza went cold. Weight settled over her limbs as if she were made of lead. Of course, she'd been foolish. Who *had* said anything about hearts? She'd assumed something was growing between them.

"Forgive me for my mistake. I'd forgotten that you'd already told me quite some time ago in your letter that you don't have one."

"Eliza—"

About to be sick with the nauseating anguish of having been so wrong about what had been developing between them—nothing, apparently—she plowed onward. "You couldn't have done anything more scandalous. Dueling is illegal—"

"You don't think I know that?"

"You're lucky I have Corbeau for a dear friend. In his eyes, a friend of mine is a friend of his. You'll have to thank him later for the fact that you won't be driven out of England. All you've worked for would have been left in the hands of others. It's practically like you were ready to throw it all away."

"That was the last thing I was doing. On the contrary—think what would have happened to your name and reputation had he begun boasting of his exploits."

"That leads directly back to decisions again. Specifically, how do you have the right to make that decision for us? You didn't consult me."

"A man generally doesn't before fighting a duel for his wife's honor." He grimaced and rolled his head away.

"Jeremy, I did not need your protection. I did not need vengeance, nor did I ask for it. I don't want to live in the past any longer."

"Then it's a good thing one of us considered what the impact of the scandal would have been on the family had he began talking about his exploit."

"Pardon me?" She froze. "On the *family*?"

He winced and shook his head a little, breathing deeply as if trying to block out the pain. "The scandal of what he did to you would have been far, far worse for the Landons than the scandal I'll bear for having dueled."

"Is that what this is about? The family name?" He said nothing. "I think you owe me an answer."

"What do you want me to say? That I can let it all go? You have no idea what it means to have been born a Landon."

"Perhaps not, but I'm beginning to have a pretty good idea of what it means to live inside the cage of a self-imposed prison."

"What are you talking about?"

"Choice, Jeremy. I'm talking about choice. You have a choice about how you're going to live, what you're going to say, and the actions you're going to take. What you don't have a choice in is what people *say* about you."

"What does that have to do with self-imposed prisons?"

She let out an exasperated sigh. "Because you don't have to live this way. You're living in fear and motivated by fear. All you've done since you inherited your title is live your life in the wake of a scandal that wasn't your own."

"And I very well don't want to live in the wake of yet *another* scandal that wasn't of my own making."

They sat together in tense silence.

It was a long time before she could speak again. "I've never felt more alone than I do now."

For some reason, she needed him to know.

"What are you talking about?" He scowled. "I'm right here."

"That's the trouble, isn't it? You're here, but that's not enough for me. I'm not going to hide my feelings. Not anymore, and certainly not with you. Whom would I be protecting? You? That's not fair to me."

"Those are dangerous words, my lady."

"Good. I won't shy away from them. And I won't shy away from this, either. I deserve better than what you are willing to give me."

• • •

Jeremy's mind spun. What use would his heart be if he went and got it shot through?

She was right. He was being a stubborn ass trying to argue with her. He'd spent so many years working—all to the detriment of a life. A real life, with love and laughter, companionship and intimacy.

Moreover, she did deserve better. Better than him. Better than his paltry excuses designed to keep her at arm's length. Designed to prevent himself from acknowledging the bond growing between them.

If he survived this, he would never choose work over living ever again. He would resume his violin and play every day. Take long walks in the gardens. Restore the orangery to its former glory. Make love to his wife in the afternoon.

Why had he written that stupid nonsense about his heart? Force of ludicrous habit? It was like he'd been trying to protect himself. And from what? Admitting that he'd made a mistake? Or was he trying to protect himself from something far more dangerous?

He covered his face with his hands and heard the airy swish of Eliza's garments as she stood, the soft treads over thick carpet, the door to the drawing room opening. And the click of it shutting again.

"Eliza?" But, of course, no answer came.

At least not the one he wanted. As to his assertion whether or not he had a heart, that place in the center of his chest was proving him the world's worst liar. If he hadn't one, there would be no pain. Jeremy had no description for what he felt, except that being shot in the arm and stitched up afterward was nothing—*nothing*—if he lost Eliza forever.

What have I done?

Chapter Thirty-Four

A week later, Eliza was in Grace's drawing room with Hetty. It was a gray day. Rain spattered the windows, and the sound of carriage wheels splashing through standing water could be heard from the streets. The same as every other day since she'd walked out of Jeremy's house. She stabbed at her embroidery.

A servant entered. "Another message arrived for Lady Bennington."

Eliza didn't need to raise her eyes to know the sort of look Grace was giving her.

Grace collected the note herself and sent the maid away. In a whispering rustle of light skirts, she went to the mantel and added it to the growing pile. "I'll put it here with the others."

Without another word, Grace buried herself back in the publication she'd been perusing, *Description de l'Égypte*.

"That's the third one today." Hetty gave Eliza a gentle nudge.

"The fourth, actually. And no, I don't plan to read it." If there had been a fire going, Eliza would have taken matters into her own hands.

If the earl could pen so many notes, he must be healing with miraculous alacrity.

Eliza stabbed her needle back into the fabric, lancing herself quite by accident. "Ow!"

Apparently embroidering while agitated was hazardous.

She brought her wounded finger to her mouth—and memories flashed back to that day in her mother's drawing room when she'd done the exact same thing. It had been right before she'd decided how she was going to save Christiana.

Daisy took the opportunity to nose under Eliza's arm and settle herself on her mistress's lap, staring up at her with mournful brown eyes.

Eliza held the dog close. That day Jeremy had given her Daisy, he hadn't yet known she'd deceived him. She'd never forget how he'd looked at her when he'd studied her from the threshold before she let on she knew he was there. Or his expression that morning when Sir Domnall had baited him before the duel.

Eliza had been silent for a full week. Her friends had politely skirted any dangerous matters, limiting discourse to polite topics. Nothing one couldn't say in the company of, say, one of the patronesses of Almack's. The weather came up with more regularity than in normal conversation, especially normal conversation between friends. And it was always rather strained. There was only so much one could belabor the subject of rain, even when one was English.

They were taking her lead. Allowing her whatever room and time she needed before she broached talking about Jeremy or the duel.

A week was long enough.

Eliza could stay silent no longer. "Don't you think it's wrong for a man who claims to be so highly concerned about scandal to go off and fight a *duel*, of all things?"

Grace and Hetty gave her near-identical solemn expressions. Then they shared a glance. Hetty chewed her lip a moment before speaking. "You make it sound as if he *wanted* to fight a duel. He did it on *your* behalf. That is to say, he was *forced* to do so, on your behalf."

"I told him *not* to fight."

"Aren't you worth the scandal of a duel?"

It had been an innocent enough question—at least that's what Eliza was going to believe. She couldn't lift her gaze from her embroidery to try to search her friend's face for clues. "That's not the point."

But was it part of the puzzle? Those ugly things Sir Domnall had said—did some part of her believe them to be true? Captain Pearson had.

The point was, she deserved love. She'd learned it far too late, when she'd already fallen quite badly in love with Jeremy. The only love she wanted now was his. But he'd never promised her his heart. Quite the opposite, from the earliest days.

Somewhere between the morning of the duel and the aftermath, the scandal had become secondary. It had become about them. About whether they could survive together *without* love between them. Hers alone wasn't enough.

And she already had her answer to that.

Remembering his words, her pulse started to pound. Prickling heat bloomed in her eyes, the sort that portended tears. Not again. Please, not again.

I am not going to cry. I am not going to cry. I am not going to cry.

She needed to regain control over her emotions. Jeremy couldn't love her. In the beginning, it hadn't mattered.

Now it was the only thing that did.

When would it stop hurting?

Lord Corbeau burst into the drawing room. "Change of

plans for tonight, ladies. There's a ball. We're going. Be sure to take particular care in your…" He gestured helplessly. "Well, you know."

Eliza demurred. "Oh, I don't think I'm ready—"

"Especially you, Lady Bennington."

"I've been so terribly weary lately and not feeling particularly well, and—"

"All this moping about, that's what it is. It's not good for one's health. You need cheering, and I intend to see that you are cheered."

Because they had been friends for so long, Eliza was familiar with the earl's gruff ways. Social interactions didn't come easily to him, even among those with whom he was closest.

Grace rose. "Are we all going, my love?"

"Yes. All of us. Even me. Scandal or no scandal, we're not going to allow what is being said about us to drive us into hiding."

With that, he left.

There was a long silence.

Eliza licked her lips. About the last thing in the world she wanted to do was go to a ball. "I really don't think I can see anyone."

"He's right, though." Resuming her seat, Grace spoke gently. "We can't let what is being said drive us into hiding or influence our actions. I thought that was important once, too. It's not."

"He might've said *us*, but he meant *me*." Idly, Eliza rubbed the wound on her finger. It'd stopped bleeding but remained sore.

Hetty smiled. "Yes, but we're guilty by association. Which is good for me, because I want to be guilty of something, and I'm so rarely presented with the proper opportunities. Properly improper opportunities, that is."

Grace gave her a look. "And just what would you do with an improper opportunity?"

"Take advantage of my good luck, of course."

"If your brother heard you talking this way—"

"He can pretend he has a say in what I do." Hetty's grin widened. "But I wouldn't mind stirring up a little scandal for myself. I wouldn't mind in the least."

Improper opportunities. Those were all well and good. But Eliza's place was doing the right thing—the *proper* thing—whether the person she had in mind deserved it or not.

Taking Daisy in her arms, Eliza pushed to her feet. "I need to see my mother."

"Oh, no, please." Grace looked at her imploringly. "Don't leave. It's a ball. I'm sure it's going to be as dull as every other one we've ever been to, and it will surely do us all good to have a night to get our minds off this business."

Hetty frowned. "I don't think balls are dull."

Grace *tsked* at her.

Eliza glanced between the two. "You must admit that a ball is the last place in the world to get our minds off this business. Everyone will be talking."

"So let's show them that we don't care what they're saying." Hetty looked hopeful.

Eliza nodded. "I agree wholeheartedly, but your words don't only apply to me. Have your husband send directions to my mother's house. We'll be there."

"We?"

"I can't go without her. She's wallowing in shame." And the thing about shame was, if one let it eat one away, there would be nothing left. Eliza had lived with her own shame for long enough. "If I'm going to show people I don't care, I need her by my side."

Chapter Thirty-Five

Jeremy's nerves were knotted beyond hope. The wound on his arm ached. Under his jacket, he still wore a bandage to keep the blood and salve from ruining his linen shirts.

If Eliza would but come…

Grace stood by his side, bolstering his courage. "She promised us she'd be here."

He'd convinced Lady Delamore to open her house to them for the night. It hadn't taken much to sway her into agreeing. First, he'd promised that the burden of the planning would be his and his alone, and he'd pay every expense himself. Second, when he'd told her the purpose of the gathering, her eyes had gone wide.

One generally did not throw balls of this magnitude without weeks of detailed planning. Jeremy had quickly found out that he'd undertaken more than he'd bargained for. But the only thing that mattered was Eliza. So he'd worked around the clock, hired help, and bribed handsomely where extra incentive was required. The efforts had paid off.

Accruing scandal after scandal in so short a time span had

positioned Jeremy rather well in one regard—people were hungry to see and hear what one of *those notorious Landons* would do next.

Except one person was missing. The most important of all. He swallowed, the agony of knowing he'd lost her forever because of his own foolishness was too much to bear. "She's not coming."

The receiving line had dwindled to nothing, and there were no stragglers in sight.

"If you'd let us tell her—"

"Then she *never* would have agreed to come."

Just as they were turning to go to the ballroom themselves and officially begin the night, two figures appeared beyond the open door.

His heart leaped. She *had* come. By her side was her mother. Lady Rushworth glared. But he could muster no energy for complaint. Eliza had come.

Catching sight of him, she visibly faltered and pulled back a little. Seeming to remember herself, she lowered her gaze and ventured the rest of the way inside.

She gave Grace a look but held her tongue. Ever so slightly, Grace lifted one shoulder.

They were remaining silent on account of Lady Delamore standing beside them, of course. She was a tiny woman, practically miniature, but her sparkling eyes missed nothing. Least of all the silent exchange between the known friends and confidantes, Lady Bennington and Lady Corbeau.

With a gloved hand, Eliza undid the ribbon of her cloak. The long swathe of fabric fell away. About her throat were glinting pale-yellow diamonds.

They were beautiful, and not the least out of place in such environs. He wouldn't have thought much about them were it not for Lady Rushworth's reaction. She inhaled a sharp breath, hand flying to cover her mouth. She didn't blink, only stared at the stones.

Eliza noticed her mother's expression and reached up to touch the jewelry. "What is it, Mother?"

"Where—where did you get those?"

Beside him, both Grace and Lady Delamore leaned in closer, hanging on every word.

Eliza seemed not to notice. "Father gave them to me."

"They were supposed to be for *me*."

"Do you want them?"

"No, I don't want them. Your father, fool that he was, gave them to that good-for-nothing old Lord Bennington"—she shot Jeremy a murderous look and sneered—"*your uncle*, and I never saw them again."

Eliza spoke gently. "But if they mean something to you, Mother—"

"They mean nothing to me but disgrace and dishonor." Lady Rushworth's mouth set. She turned to Jeremy and pointed to the stones. "This was your debt, my lord."

He blinked, no comprehension forming in his mind. "What? What do these have to do with the debt? That was a jewel—"

"*Jewels.*" Her mouth pinched as if the mere act of speaking to him was more distasteful than anything else imaginable. "Have another look at whatever it is to which you were referring. I believe you missed a small detail, my lord."

"A small detail?"

"The *S* at the end of the word, I think you'll find."

That had to have been why nobody had ever been able to trace the item. He'd had runners trying to find a jewel. Not a set of jewels.

Eliza's mouth parted. "Then he never had to marry me."

Jeremy was dimly mindful of the servants closing the front doors and of Grace dragging Lady Delamore away while the older woman was still trying to crane her neck to watch what was unfolding.

But the awareness of the pain in her words crowded out most everything else. They put a dagger into his heart.

Lady Rushworth, however, hadn't moved. "Still time for an annulment."

"Mother, please."

"You had a hand in this, my lady." Jeremy struggled to keep his tone reasonably civil. She was still his mother-in-law, after all. He intended to see to it that was what she remained. For better or for worse… "If you hadn't tried to force me to marry Christiana, your daughter and I never would have met."

The anguish of the thought made it difficult to breathe. Never met Eliza…never met the one person in the world who meant more to him than any other.

"Are you trying to blame *my daughter* for this? Disgraceful."

Eliza gave her husband a hard look. "It seems you're blaming my mother. Why don't we all agree to drop the subject of who is responsible for what? We're in this now, whether we like it"—she swallowed, lowering her eyes, as if she suffered some deep internal struggle—"or not. Either way, we're going to have to come to terms with what our situation is. Mother, you're destitute. You're going to need a place to live, so you're going to have to decide between coming to Idlewood with us or going to the dower house."

Jeremy braced himself. He was going to have to live with Lady Rushworth. It seemed a small price to pay for keeping Eliza. Idlewood was large. If he ate separately at breakfast and during the day, and accepted invitations to dine with families in the neighborhood, they had only to endure each other over the occasional dinner.

Lady Rushworth drew a long breath. "Still time for an annulment, I say."

Beside her, Eliza's cheeks went red. "I'm afraid it's rather too late to consider that, Mother."

"I know you keep saying that, Eliza, but you must listen to reason—"

"No, I mean because I'm beginning to suspect there is going to be a child."

The conversation came to an abrupt halt as they both stared at her.

Eliza's cheeks darkened. "I thought you would be more pleased, my lord. It's what you wanted from marriage."

Pleased? The weight of the world had settled upon his shoulders. And it was so much heavier than he ever could have believed. What if it was a boy? He'd have his heir—but would he have Eliza? But what if it was a girl? How could he live with himself knowing there were predators like Sir Domnall slithering through the world who would prey upon loneliness and a tender heart?

He'd thought he'd felt protective of Eliza before. It was *nothing* to what he was experiencing now, for both her and the life they'd created.

It was too much. A child. *A child!* It wasn't supposed to feel like this, was it? The best thing in the world. He'd never been lighter. Or so frightened. Ice chilled his entire being. What if Eliza didn't survive childbirth?

No. He couldn't think about that. Not now. Maybe not ever. If he lost her…

His throat closed.

Jeremy's determination redoubled. No child of his was going to be raised in a house where there was any question of whether the mother and father loved each other.

And what was that last bit? A child was what he'd wanted from a marriage? Maybe in the beginning. Now…well, yes, of course he wanted children. He wanted them very much. But it was so much more complex now.

No. It wasn't. He wanted *her*. Eliza. His wife. His dear one—the one who taught him more about what it was to love than he'd ever imagined could possibly exist. If he was hopeless now, so be it. He didn't want to return to what he'd been before he knew her.

He must win her tonight once and for all. Nothing else mattered.

"Come. We have a ball to begin. Mustn't keep the people waiting."

Chapter Thirty-Six

Eliza was not prepared for what happened when Jeremy led her into the ballroom.

First, he left her on the sidelines with her mother. They were standing with Corbeau, Grace, and Hetty. Jeremy's hands went up, and everyone moved aside, emptying the floor to give the man command of the room. Silence fell.

"Ladies and gentlemen. Thank you for coming tonight on such very short notice." Jeremy turned, studying the company but carefully avoiding meeting Eliza's eye.

Lady Rushworth tapped Eliza's arm with her fan. "What is he doing?" she whispered.

"I don't know." She shook her head and looked at Grace—who also avoided her gaze. Hetty shot Eliza a wide smile and an encouraging nod.

Jeremy continued. "Many of you have heard rumors about members of my family lately. Some of them are true. Some of them are not. Think what you choose, of course. None of us are going to confirm or deny anything."

A murmur went through the crowd. Disappointment,

perhaps?

"That said, there are a few items I would like you all to be the first to know about."

Eliza's heart started pounding. Her mother grabbed her arm. "What does that husband of yours think he's doing? He's going to disgrace us all."

"*Shh.*"

"Whatever you heard about my wedding, forget it this instant." Jeremy paused to take a deep breath. Every last person in the room was waiting for him to speak. He lowered his head as if he were drawing courage for what he had to say next. He raised it again, his face stony with whatever it took inside him to account for himself, while his voice was hard with the determination of a man resolved not to reveal too much emotion. "Once I wrote to my wife that I didn't have a heart. No sooner did she show me that I do than it became hers, wholly and irrevocably."

At last, their eyes met. Lord, he really was declaring himself before the world. If he said any more…

Oh, no. Not again. I am not going to cry. I am not going to cry. I am not going to cry.

"Eliza, I love you." He looked away, the private moment between them in a very public place broken, as he returned to addressing the crowd. "I explicitly forbid any and every person here from ever discussing any of us Landons ever again. If not for us, then—"

His gaze found Eliza again, his brows lifting in silent question. Words weren't necessary to understand the question. She blinked away the wetness in her eyes, and he responded with a single nod.

"Ladies and gentlemen, I have the very great pleasure of announcing that in a few short months…" He paused to raise his eyes to the high ceiling a moment, clearly making a quick mental calculation. "Come late January or early February, I'd guess, my wife and I will be welcoming our first child into the world."

The room erupted into cheers.

Hetty gasped. "I'm going to be an aunt again!"

"Again?" Was there a secret half sibling in the family that Eliza didn't know about?

Grace pulled Eliza into an embrace, whispering in her ear, "Our children will be very nearly the same age."

Eliza stepped back. Grace veritably glowed. She and Corbeau shared a look. If Eliza didn't know better, she might have said a touch of color came into Corbeau's cheeks. He cleared his throat, as stiff and awkward as ever. "I think this is my cue to go make myself useful inspecting the books in the Delamore library. I've heard tell they have several particularly rare volumes that I've been wanting to study."

Grace waved at him. "You go on then. We'll be all right."

He leaned over to place a little kiss on her cheek. "Don't overtire yourself, my love. Send a servant when you're ready to depart."

Not seeming entirely conscious of doing so, Eliza pressed her hand to her belly. There was as yet no outward sign of the impending event. But that would come.

Men were coming forward to shake Jeremy's hand, offering their congratulations. He accepted them graciously and then pushed through the crowd to offer his hand to Eliza.

"Shall we open the ball?"

Their fingers came together. He led her to the floor. Other couples came to join them on the line. Jeremy nodded to the waiting musicians.

The music began.

"You can't stop them from talking, you know."

"I know. That wasn't so much my aim as trying to prove to you that I'm worthy. That I'm going to work each and every day to be the husband you deserve. That I can set aside the petty concerns of others. Frankly, I wish I had sooner. But it took you coming into my life before I realized what was important."

Eliza had no answer.

When the dance was over, they slipped out onto the terrace. The night was warm and clear, filled with the scent of the rain that had fallen that afternoon and the soaked blossoms. Overhead hung countless stars, more beautiful than all the gemstones the world over.

They stood together in a moment of silence before he turned to her, an unusual vulnerability in his features. "I'm sorry for those dreadfully stupid things I said after the duel. And for the duel itself. You were right. All my life I've tried to keep myself in check. But I wanted to kill him. Seeing him with you—but I won't try to offer excuses for my actions. I was wrong. You were right. My anger got the better of me. I can only hope you will, in time, begin to forgive me."

"Forgive you?" It was her turn to be vulnerable. "Jeremy, I love you. You only ever need ask and my forgiveness is yours."

He softened. "I shall endeavor not to need to ask for it."

"We're human. We make mistakes. Plenty of them, all of us, and we all need forgiveness. From ourselves and from others. Whenever you need it from me, I will give it. Never be afraid to ask."

"I don't deserve you."

She put her arms around his neck and tilted her head as their lips drew closer. "Good thing that doesn't matter. Because you have me. From this moment forward, we'll be united to face whatever comes our way."

He ran his hand down her back. "Forever."

"Forever. And I'm never leaving your side."

Their mouths met. He pulled away to whisper in her ear, "You'll never be alone again."

She smiled. "That's because I have Daisy."

It felt good to be playful. The past was finally falling away, because the present was more than she ever could have dreamed. The only thing that mattered any longer was what they did now and in the future. Not what they'd done a week, a month, or a year ago.

Jeremy swatted her backside. She yelped and giggled. "And me, wife. Don't think I'm ever going to let you forget it."

Epilogue

Christmas Day, two and a half years later

"How did she get ahold of this?" Jeremy, sitting on the rumpled covers of the bed, took a sparkling diamond earring from his daughter's tiny fist. Lady Mary squealed in outrage as her father took her pretty prize, then fell into a peal of giggles as he began tickling her. The child had her mother's dark hair and her father's large aquamarine eyes. "I thought you kept them locked away."

They were enjoying a lazy family morning in the bedchamber Eliza and Jeremy shared at Idlewood. Mary had woken and nursed before slipping from the bed to toddle about exploring.

Eliza tried not to smile as she took the jewelry from her husband. One of the unexpected realities of motherhood was trying not to laugh when her child found her way into mischief. "I must have forgotten."

"Do you remember the night of the ball?"

"Which one?" She crossed the room and found the box

open on the dressing table. Mary must have crawled up on the chair and helped herself. Little imp.

"You know—when I stood up like a stuffy old popinjay and told people not to gossip."

"You're certainly stuffy and old, my dear, but calling yourself a popinjay is going a bit far." Eliza smiled as she teased her husband. "But yes, I remember."

"Were you really going to hand the jewels over to your mother?"

Mary had freed herself from her father's grasp and was running toward her mother with her arms up. Daisy followed, gleefully scampering behind, tail wagging with mad joy.

Ironically, although "Papa" had been one of Mary's first words, she had yet to say "Mama." Never mind that she preferred to spend the greater portion of her day attached to her mother.

Mary's tiny shift was askew, revealing her chubby legs. Eliza scooped the child into her arms. "If she'd wanted them, certainly. I'd have given them to her then and there." She gave him a curious look. "Why are you thinking about this now?"

He shrugged. "An errant thought, is all."

"She can still have them if she wants them. All she has to do is ask."

"But she won't."

Mary's birth had had an unexpected side effect that neither of them had anticipated. For all of Lady Rushworth's failings as a mother, she didn't seem to have any failings as a grandmother.

Which they both saw evidence of when the trio entered the Idlewood breakfast room. Lady Rushworth, fingers bare of all adornment but for a simple gold wedding band, abandoned her kippers to sweep the small girl up and twirl her around. Jeremy and Eliza shared what had to have been their thousandth look since their daughter's birth and shook their heads. Who was this woman and what had she done with Lady Rushworth? Sometimes she went a whole week without uttering the word "disgraceful." Not even under her breath. They'd considered senility to be at the root of the change, but her mind seemed as sharp as ever.

When Jeremy and Eliza had advertised for a nurse, Lady Rushworth had deemed none of the applicants worthy of the charge. More amazing was that Jeremy's part in Mary's creation had won him a begrudging truce with the woman. There was no question she still wasn't happy he'd married her daughter. But she no longer seemed to hold his mere existence against him.

Also at the breakfast table were Corbeau and Grace, their daughter, Lady Amelia, on her father's lap, rosebud mouth ringed with jam from raspberries grown year-round in the restored Idlewood orangery, the table around her covered in smears and crumbs. Daisy was grateful for both Amelia's and Mary's unrefined meal practices and stood vigil under their chairs to ensure that the servants didn't have the bother of cleaning the floor. She…he…she was a very considerate dog.

After a long day of festivities, Jeremy pinched out the candle and collapsed in bed beside Eliza, too tired to move. Mary was already asleep between them, having nursed to sleep, and was sprawled as only a small child can sprawl. "I didn't know Christmas could be quite so *loud*."

Two years ago, his hand would have ached for having played the violin as long as he had today. Today, he almost didn't notice. The musical selection had been a deft mix of lighthearted and enthusiastic improvisations to delight the children and a few more studied pieces for the adults' pleasure.

Though it was dark, he could hear the smile in Eliza's

response. "I shouldn't wonder if it were louder next year."

Jeremy's eyes popped open. She wasn't telling him... "You mean because of Corbeau and Grace's new addition?"

He couldn't breathe while he waited for her answer. It seemed an eternity coming.

"Theirs...and ours, too."

The same dizzying array of emotions he couldn't fully catalog clutched his heart, as when she'd told him she was expecting Mary. Weren't these things supposed to become easier with practice? After seeing Eliza through childbirth once, it was incredible she wanted to endure it again. That said, Mary herself was a strong inducement. Not because she necessarily needed a sibling, but because the naughty little mischief maker brought so much love and laughter into the house.

He decided that, for now, the only thing he needed to feel was Eliza's hand. He reached for her, lacing her fingers with his...and squeezed. She squeezed back.

Acknowledgments

This book would quite literally not have come together without my very dear friends with very large brains. The first draft of this book did not go well. With good reason, you'll find out—read to the end.

Fearing I wouldn't finish by deadline and my romance-writing career would be over before it had begun, I panicked and sought help from a number of sources. Later, when I needed help again in the eleventh hour of my first deadline, a number of them stepped up again. Several months later, after having scrapped the entire draft and started again nearly from scratch, I had yet more help.

Thank you to Marta Miller Bliese for asking critical questions of the first (failed) draft, pointing out issues of dire concern, and helping me refocus on the bigger picture instead of the collective (disjointed) parts. Thank you a second time for not falling asleep reading a partially finished draft of that same ol' failed manuscript, and for your wickedly spot-on feedback. Thank you yet again (!) for reading the first chapter after I came to my senses (adding Christiana and the epistolary element) and letting me know I'd finally found my stride with the story and characters. Thank you for everything you've done for me and will continue to do. Please start writing again and don't give up hope. You're an incredible talent. I think about your stories every day.

Thank you to Laurel Wanrow for swooping in without hesitation when she had so much else on her very full plate and while regaining her footing after a setback of her own. Laurel and I were sisters living under the (very real) Curse of Book Three, and we're alive to tell the tale. Thank you for all your help and advice. I miss our library time!

Thank you to Miguelina Perez for doing a rush read on the first (failed) draft when I'd been stuck for days. Thank you for loving the characters and being so supportive. Thank you for brainstorming to get me unstuck. Thank you for beta reading the draft that eventually became this book. Having you in my corner bolsters me when times are tough.

Thank you to Adele Buck, who texted me after seeing a note on Facebook and offered to help, encouraging me to allow the characters to mess up more.

An extra big thank-you to the brilliant calls-it-like-she-sees-it Christi Barth. She's been extremely—*extremely*—generous to me with her time and expertise. She has helped me time and again. Selflessly, too. There is no way I can ever thank this woman enough or pay her back for what she's done; I only hope I can pay it forward someday. Christi, I hope you enjoy the character named in your honor (though she's quite different from you) and the love story I gave her in the book to reflect your own in a very small way. Thank you for matchmaking so M. C. Vaughn and I could find each other.

Thank you to my two new critique partners, M.C. Vaughn and Carrie Lomax, for support, encouragement, coffee, lunches, insightful comments, and endless hilarity.

Thank you to Meghan Maslow, Carla Coupe, and again

to Adele, who read the first fifty pages of the failed version of this story in critique group and offered advice. Though I scrapped that draft (rightly so—it was awful), your insights and questions helped me learn and grow.

The romance-writing community is an incredible group of talent and support. I'm humbled to be a part of this group. I hope what I do, how I act, and what I write reflect well on all of you when my books go out into the world.

And to my beta readers, Linda E. and Nicole R. from Goodreads, Mary D. from Facebook, and my RWA friends, Katrina Sizemore, Miguelina Perez (again), and Carrie Lomax (again). You all helped immeasurably.

Thank you to the team at Entangled. Each and every one of you has been incredible to work with. A shout-out to Holly Bryant-Simpson for seeing on Instagram I was in Atlanta and getting in touch so we could meet and chat. I can't wait to see you again!

But most especially my editor, Erin Molta, whose smarts have helped me grow as a writer as she gently but firmly guided these manuscripts into their final form with kindness, insight, and warmth. (Including another late-in-the-game *major* revision.) Thank you for what you bring to the world with these amazing books.

If this story works, it's only because I received no-nonsense guidance from these talented people. If it doesn't, the failing is wholly my own.

Thank you again to the lovely Geraldine, my son's former babysitter—we miss you! And to the vivacious and readerly Emily, his new babysitter. To Jamaila Brinkley, for our babysitting co-op, all our talks, and the pretzels she allowed me to pilfer when I wandered through her kitchen absently mulling over plot points, dialogue, and how to realize the dark moments and grand gestures Erin Molta patiently guided me toward.

I also have to give a shout-out to Sherri LaRowe, our Realtor, who saw us through real estate trauma and drama with grace, humor, and a special kind of brilliance. Maybe that's why the first draft of this story had no conflict—I had too much in real life! Nobody is savvier or harder working than Sherri. She is nothing short of a living, walking, breathing blessing—in every sense of the word. (The Silver Lion Inn near Idlewood is named after the silver spray-painted lion statue she and I saw next door to the first house my husband and I tried to buy.)

Most of all, thank you to the man himself, my beloved husband, Jonathan, for his hard work, support, and indefatigable sense of humor, even when he's turning a pithy phrase at the expense of what a duke might do with his you know what.

About the Author

Ingrid Hahn is a failed administrative assistant with a B.A. in Art History. Her love of reading has turned her mortgage payment into a book storage fee, which makes her the friend who you never want to ask you for help moving. Though originally from Seattle, she now lives in the metropolitan DC area with her ship-nerd husband, small son, and four opinionated cats. When she's not reading or writing, she loves knitting, theater, nature walks, travel, history, and is a hopelessly devoted fan of Jane Austen. Please connect with her on social media! Find her on Twitter as @Ingrid_Writer, on Instagram as ingrid_hahn, and on Facebook as Ingrid Hahn.

Discover the* Landon Sisters *series…

To Win a Lady's Heart

To Covet a Lady's Heart

Get Scandalous with these historical reads…

The Duke Meets His Match

an *Infamous Somertons* novel by Tina Gabrielle

Chloe Somerton grew up poor. Desperate to aid her sisters, she'd picked a pocket…or two. Now Chloe has a chance to marry a young, wealthy lord. Only his mentor—a dark, dangerous duke—stands in her way. The duke knows about her past, and she'll do anything to keep him from telling. What begins as a battle of wills soon escalates into a fierce attraction…

Denying the Duke

a *Lords and Ladies in Love* novel by Callie Hutton

Alex returns to assume the title Duke of Bedford when his brother unexpectedly dies. He is unprepared for both his new responsibilities and the reunion with Patience, the woman he'd loved who had been betrothed to his brother. He has been to war and is a changed man. Doesn't Patience know that! Where is the man she loved gone? They must accept the changes or deny them and move on.

The Twelve Days of Seduction

by Maire Claremont

Alexander Hunt, Eighth Duke of Berresford, is aware his ward's governess, Adriana Flint, misrepresented herself to gain employment, and he's quite displeased, even if she is one of the most intelligent women's he's ever met. Desperate to convince the sexy duke not to tear her from the little girl she's grown to adore, Adriana challenges him to prove she's not the reputable governess he believed he hired. If he can seduce her before the Twelve Days of Christmas have come to an end, she will leave without protest. But when they find the challenge more difficult than either imagined, can they face the consequences of their decisions?

Undercover with the Earl

a *Brotherhood of the Sword* novel by Robyn DeHart

The arrogant Earl of Somersby, Bennett Haile, is far more vested in protecting the Queen than finding a wife. For he has the perfect tool with which to lure out the villains…a young woman with an uncanny likeness to the queen. Under his tutelage, country girl Evelyn Marrington will have to fool the entire court that she is, in fact, the queen. But as danger threatens from every side, Bennett's lovely little protegé isn't just placing her life in his hands…she's stealing his heart.

Made in the USA
Middletown, DE
23 June 2017